HOLES
IN THE
GROUND

A Dan Courtwright Mystery

Other Books by Paul Wagner :

Dan Courtwright Mysteries
Danger: Falling Rocks
Bones of the Earth

Artisan Public Relations
Wine Sales and Distribution
Wine Marketing and Sales

Lecture Series:
The Instant Sommelier (Great Courses)
A History of Wine in 10 Glasses (Audible)

HOLES
IN THE
GROUND

PAUL WAGNER

A Dan Courtwright Mystery

Published by Albicaulis Books

For Margaret, forever

BONES OF THE EARTH

prologue

The impact of mining in the Sierra foothills is no longer immediately obvious to the casual observer. True, there are state parks that preserve some of the older buildings, and even a couple that preserve the mining operations themselves. But the impact on the landscape is now slowly fading into the misty past.

That's true, unless you take the time to stop and look at what you are seeing. Because the evidence is all around you. And it is overwhelming.

Driving from the San Francisco Bay Area to the foothills of the Gold Country, you drive through the massive delta of the Sacramento and San Joaquin Rivers, some of the richest farmland in the world. But stop for a moment to consider the water level of the rivers and compare it to the surrounding farmland. The detritus from hydraulic mining washed down those rivers and raised their beds far above where they were 200 years ago. That sediment also filled in a substantial part of San Francisco Bay.

As you drive through the small Gold Country towns in California, take a look alongside the riverbeds in those towns. Often you will see huge piles of boulders and cobblestones, all removed from the riverbed by miners who were hoping to find nuggets, or at least gold-bearing sediment, underneath them.

And as you hike through the foothills you will often find these tailings far from current towns. The population of the foothills today is far different than it was in the 1850s, and what we think of as unoccupied canyons were sometimes bustling mining areas back then. Only the piles of tailings, and a few rusty pots or nails, bear evidence to their previous life.

While early gold miners focused on panning for nuggets in the rivers and streams of the Sierra, later miners used massive hydraulic systems to wash entire mountains through sluicing tunnels and down into the Sacramento River and San Francisco Bay. Such mining led to a landmark legal decision, the Sawyer Decision, in 1884, often considered the first environmental impact decision in the world.

San Francisco Bay became shallower as a result of the 1.5 billion cubic yards of debris washed down from the hydraulic mines. And mercury contamination from these same mines is a water quality issue in the bay even today, roughly 150 years after the Sawyer Decision.

What was the source of all that rock and gravel? Most of it came from ancient riverbeds that had been uplifted into the Sierra Foothills over millions of years. While miners who panned for gold looked for it in the sediments of the current rivers, hydraulic mining aimed to find the source of that gold, in the bottoms of ancient riverbeds now buried deep in the dry foothills. It was a vastly more industrial scale of mining.

To wash that sediment out of the hills, entire rivers were redirected, and flumes constructed to take water far from its natural course. You can still see these flumes and ditches in many parts of the Sierra foothills—some of which are still maintained to carry water as part of a local water district. They are living traces of our gold mining past.

But the most sought-after of all gold discoveries was not the nuggets in the riverbed, nor even the rich gravels of ancient rivers. The true Holy Grail for some miners was the Mother Lode: the vein of hard rock that contained the rich gold deposits where they formed, in the native rock, before being washed down into river sediments. And to get to that gold, you had to dig into hard rock.

Tens of thousands of mines were dug into the Sierra Foothills in search of gold. The official estimate is somewhere around 40,000 to 60,000 mines, and thousands of roads were constructed to bring the equipment to those mines. Today you can see some of that equipment on display in just about every town in the Gold Country. But you can also find it littered throughout the landscape of the foothills, sometimes in the yard of a homeowner, sometimes sitting abandoned on the side of a hill, or virtually hidden in the underbrush of a remote canyon.

It is everywhere. And so are the mines.

In fact, in 2000, the State of California commissioned a study of these abandoned mines and the dangers they present. The study found more than 125,000 mining features in California and estimated that roughly 50,000 of these features included hazardous openings.

About half of these are on federal land, and most of the rest are on private land. Only about 2% are on State of California land. After the Great Recession of 2008-10, the American Recovery and Reinvestment Act invested tens of millions of dollars in locating and filling some of these mines. The goal was to reduce the danger to people and wildlife, because these shafts are usually unmarked, unprotected, and of unknown depth. But the impact was, admittedly, minimal.

While money is always an issue, the other problem is knowing where all these mines were located and how to access them. Private landowners often harbor a secret hope that someday they might re-open their mine and are unwilling to have the federal government identify just exactly where it is. And such mines might well be considered an attractive nuisance by insurance companies unwilling to pay for injuries to those who trespass on the private property to explore them.

Mines on federal land are even less well-known. "You can imagine that gold miners back in the 1860s didn't want people to know where their gold mines were," says Office of Mine Reclamation Spokesperson Don Drysdale. "They didn't exactly write these things down or map them out very well. So, we're still finding them all the time." *

Yes, we are.

The town of Sonora, a gateway to Yosemite National Park, is honeycombed with mines. As an article by Nicholas Beale on the Untapped New York website explains nicely, "Sonora's claim to fame as a gold rush town revolves around its extensive network of mines and shafts, which permeate the earth beneath in an area vaster than the current city. Many of the buildings that stand on Washington Street today have been constructed on pylons, or support structures." Many of the buildings have mine entrances or equipment buried in the cellar, where they become part of the foundation, both physical and spiritual, of the town.

We once drew a circle with a radius of one mile around a single point in an area of the foothills above Sonora. In researching that area, we discovered that there were seven recognized mines within that circle. Two of them have shafts that are still open—although we had enough common sense not to enter them. But one was massive: a 300-foot inclined shaft with 3 drift adits 1,500, 800 and 400 feet long. And all that was connected in the old days via an overhead cable tram. Two more are clearly on private land, and not accessible without trespassing. Two more look as if they have been filled in—but we have not explored them extensively to make sure.

And one we haven't found.

There are still gold mines operating in the Sierra foothills today. You'll find that open mining claims in these counties don't number in the tens and twenties, but in the hundreds for each county. There is, in fact, even an active claim in Yosemite National Park.

Small operators run floating dredges in the rivers, or pan for gold the old-fashioned way. But hydraulic mining still continues, albeit with significant environmental restrictions, and hard rock miners still tunnel into the rock and hillsides in search of gold-bearing veins deep in the bowels of the Earth.

There are tens of thousands of holes in the ground in the Sierra foothills. And more are being mined today. The evidence is there, if you know where to look.

*Quote from Motherlode News, June 11, 2011

HOLES IN THE GROUND

chapter 1

This was not the way Dan had wanted to spend the morning. A meeting with "all of the regulatory agencies" was absolutely as dreary as it sounds. There had been endless presentations about traffic calming practices, inter-agency cooperation, and management policies from the California Highway Patrol, the sheriff's offices of three different counties, plus local police departments and Dan's own responsibility, representing the Stanislaus National Forest. Permits, processes, and public information had all been discussed in depth.

He checked his watch and was surprised to see that it had only lasted just under two hours. If he left right now, he could be back up at the Summit Ranger Station by 11 o'clock, easy.

That's when Tuolumne County Sheriff Cal Healey caught Dan's eye, and then contorted his face into a grimace.

Dan grinned back, and Cal walked over. Twenty years ago Cal had been a pretty good college defensive back. But over the years he had added some weight to his five-foot-eleven frame, and a bad knee had added that limp. Cal always looked as if he were carrying a burden slightly heavier than anyone else's. It didn't help that he was carrying the usual paraphernalia of his office, complete with revolver, radio, and handcuffs. Dan knew how much all that weighed, and felt a twinge of pity for the Sheriff.

"Sure glad we got that all ironed out," Cal said, and then rolled his eyes in sarcasm. "There's nothing better than a bunch of government employees all trying to manage a meeting to make sure that whatever we're talking about is somebody else's problem."

Dan chuckled. "Just under two hours," he said, "Record time."

"I am going to enjoy all the overtime I'll put in up there at the pass," Cal said. "Maggie always likes it when I am gone for our Fourth of July barbecue."

"Yeah, that was pretty slick how they handed that part over to you guys," Dan agreed.

Cal snorted. "Well, they couldn't very well give it to you. Rangers managing traffic? Hell, no. Why, you boys wouldn't know what to do if you ran into two cars at a stop sign."

"We don't," Dan said with a straight face. "That's why we always just stand around and wait for you. And since you're mentioning it, I'd like to point out that it takes you a helluva long time to get there in most cases."

"Yeah, well, we have most of the county to cover," Cal said. "The CHP only gets a few roads. But, by God, they really don't want that much help on 108."

"Hey, it's the only thing they have to do," Dan replied with a nod. "They want to make sure that everybody knows they'll give out tickets in the name of safety to anyone—and everyone."

"Hell, yes. Now they've even got me to the point that I'm afraid to drive around Sonora Pass that weekend," Cal admitted, then paused. "So you think it's going to be every bit as bad as last year?"

Dan nodded. "Ever since 'Wild' came out, the numbers are higher. And with this year's lighter snowpack, a lot of people have decided this year is the year to go."

"I don't get it, really," Cal said. "A couple of thousand miles in a summer? Have you ever thought about hiking it? The whole enchilada, from Mexico to Canada?"

"Thought about it? Yes," Dan answered. "But not really. To do it in one year you have to pretty much hike straight through without stopping. That's not my style. I want to stop and check things out. But I have thought about doing it in sections, and taking my time, and exploring each section as I go."

"How long would that take you?" Cal asked.

Dan laughed. "The rest of my life."

His phone vibrated in his pocket and reminded him that he had promised Doris he would head back to the ranger station right after the meeting.

"I better get going," he said to Cal. "Doris keeps texting me about stuff."

"Sure," Cal replied. And then, paying no attention to what he had just said, he added, "Hey, how are things with Kristen?"

Dan paused. "Great! Good. I mean, it's going fine. We had dinner the other night." The dinner had ended somewhat awkwardly after a few kisses in the car in front of Kristen's house. She hadn't invited him in. Dan saw no reason to go into more detail with Cal. If there was one mystery Dan never believed he would solve, it was fully understanding the love of his life, Kristen Gallagher. But he didn't want to talk about that with Cal.

"Okay, good. That's what I can tell Maggie." Cal said. "Because you know she is going to ask me."

Dan chuckled and shook his head. "Tell her things are fine." He started walking out to his truck, thinking that "fine" wasn't really how things were. Things were confusing and complicated. But somehow Kristen continued to talk to him, and occasionally accept his invitations to dinner when she had time. At least, that's what she said.

Cal considered Dan's answer. He wasn't going to let Dan leave with that. "Fine isn't good enough for her. She wants details. And she wants it to be better than fine."

Dan stopped by the door and said, over his shoulder: "Good, tell here things are good. And that we had dinner." That was true, at any rate. And he hoped they would have many more. That was up to Kristen.

And then he hurried out the door before Cal had a chance to ask any follow-up questions.

chapter 2

Before climbing into his truck, Dan took the time to text Doris that he was on his way. He knew her well enough to know that she would fret about it until he arrived, but he hoped that this would reassure her.

He put the truck in gear and drove out of the parking lot, onto the highway. Traffic was light, and his mind began to wander back to the conversation with Cal Healey. And he wasn't thinking about the Highway Patrol or the PCT; he was thinking about Kristen.

She was really beautiful. Dan remembered her hand on the table, and the elegance of her neck. And lots of other things. He had to admit that he had no idea why she seemed to like him, but she did. It scared him a little, and it really excited him, too. He hadn't felt this way in a long time, and he wasn't sure that it was a good thing. But he certainly hoped he wasn't going to do anything to mess it up. He hoped he hadn't already done that.

Dan realized with a start that he was already at Cold Springs, only a few minutes from the ranger station. That brought him back to Doris, and why she was so persistent about today. She clearly wanted something from him, but he couldn't imagine what it was.

By the time he parked his truck around back, he was sure that she was keeping track of his progress through the windows. Dan had worked with Doris for three years now, and it was a relationship that he really valued. In the organization of the office, she worked for him, despite the fact that she was nearly old enough to be his mother and had worked in the office for more than ten years. While he had the benefit of a master's degree in forestry, her knowledge of the local area, and her ability to deal with even the most difficult people, made them a good team.

Dan did not have that ability.

"Oh, good, you're here!" Doris nearly yelled out when he walked in the door. "I know you've spent all morning at that meeting, but do you have a few minutes later today? Travis wanted to ask you some questions."

That explained it. Doris' grandson Travis was the light of her life. He was a nice kid, and doing well in school, but to hear Doris tell it, "He is simply the best young man I have ever known."

Dan smiled. "Sure. What's on his mind?"

Doris gave a sigh. "He is very interested in the Pacific Crest Trail," she said.

"Oof, that's a lot to bite off for someone still in high school," Dan said.

Doris shook her head. "No, he doesn't want to hike it. But he wants to meet someone who is hiking it."

Dan shrugged. "That's easy. Fourth of July weekend at Sonora Pass. A bunch of them will be coming through there pretty much all the time. That's why I was in Sonora today. Crowd management for the PCT on Fourth of July weekend."

"No," Doris stopped. "He wants to meet a specific person who's hiking the trail. Some computer genius or something."

Dan thought this over briefly. "That's going to be a lot harder," he said. "There's no real way of telling when each hiker is going to arrive. And some of them drop out in each section, so there's not even a guarantee that he'll make it here."

"Well, that's what I told him, Dan. But he doesn't believe his grandma. He wants to talk to the ranger."

Dan laughed. "Fine. I'm happy to tell him that at least in this case, Grandma knows exactly what she's talking about!"

Doris punched him lightly on the shoulder. "You know that's not what I mean. He just wants as much information as possible, and I thought after your meeting you might know a bit more. Besides, you know that crowd better than I do anyway."

"I'll be here all day," Dan said. "And I'm always happy to talk to Travis."

"Thanks, I'll let him know. Would two o'clock be Okay?" Doris pressed him.

"I'll put him down in my calendar," Dan said. "In ink."

Dan then spent the next two hours answering an endless stream of emails generated by the morning meeting. It seemed as if everyone at the meeting wanted to make sure that everyone else understood exactly what had been said, and who was responsible for what.

Generally, it was everybody else who was responsible. By the time two o'clock came around, Dan was happy to take a break when Travis arrived.

Dan heard Doris greet the kid with her usual glowing voice, then heard the footsteps bounce across the floor to knock on his door.

"I'll be right out!" Dan called out. He hit send on his last response to the emails, hopeful that he had put an end to at least a few of the debates that were raging, and walked out to the front counter.

Travis was now seventeen and had just finished his junior year of high school. He was not tall, maybe five foot nine, but he towered over his grandma. Freckles, red hair, and a big smile were what everyone always noticed about Travis. But Dan also knew that he was a computer whiz, and a pretty good fly-fisherman as well.

"Hey, Travis," Dan greeted him, reaching out to shake his hand. "What's up?"

"Hi…" Travis replied. He never knew whether to call the ranger Dan or Mr. Courtwright. "So I was wondering about the Pacific Crest Trail hikers…."

"Yeah," Dan helped him along. "Your grandma was telling me about that. There's somebody you want to meet?"

Travis gave a quick nod. "So do you know about Theo Willyers?" He paused.

Dan shook his head slowly. "Who is he?"

"Okay, he is a genius." Travis was almost shaking with excitement. "He's a software genius…he's the guy behind Allapp." Travis looked at Dan expectantly.

Dan smiled and shook his head, opening his hands in front of his chest. "Sorry…"

Travis nodded. "It's an app for your phone. It synchs all of your apps into a seamless system that lets you do anything you want from your phone just by telling it what to do." Travis waited to see if Dan understood this, then continued, "It's totally awesome and he's a multi-billionaire."

It was clear to Dan that Travis idolized Theo Willyers. "Wow," he said. He tried to make it sound convincing.

"I know, right?" Travis agreed. "And he dropped out of the office, completely dropped everything, because he said he wanted to take a break from everything and hike the PCT."

"That sounds like a good idea," said Dan with a smile. "I like him more now."

"I know. Cool, right? He said he's spent too much of his life in an office, and now he wants to reboot. He's gonna 'Reboot by putting some boots on the trail,'" Travis continued.

"He won't be alone in that," Dan chuckled. "There are a lot of people who seem to have that idea."

"And he's doing it in silence," Travis continued. "I mean, he's taken a vow of silence on the trail for the whole hike."

Dan smiled again as he thought about this. While most through-hikers claimed that they loved the silence and isolation of the trail, Dan had often found that they were talkative to the point of being annoying when they finally did start to talk. "I can understand that," he said.

"So I thought that I could meet him at Sonora Pass," Travis continued. "I know there are like, trail helpers that help those guys? So I thought I could help him."

"Sure, trail angels. There are people who do that, and there will be a bunch at Sonora Pass soon. But how will you know when he is going to get there?" Dan asked.

"Well, that's why I wanted to talk to you." Travis explained. "Do you have any way of tracking the PCT hikers? I mean, do they get permits in Yosemite? Could you find out when he got his permit there, and then we might figure out when he'll get to Sonora Pass."

"Not really," Dan shook his head. "And even if we could find his permit there, we still couldn't really predict when he would get to Sonora Pass. He might take a lay day somewhere, or…"

The two of them considered this in silence. Dan could feel Doris wanting to help, to say something, but there wasn't an easy solution to this one.

"There are usually somewhere between seven hundred and a

thousand hikers who do that trail every year," Dan explained. "And they all hike at a slightly different pace. It's hard to predict very much about when they will arrive where."

"Do the trail angels up at the pass have cell phones?" Doris asked. "Could they call you when he arrives?"

Travis shook his head dismissively. "Grandma, he wouldn't tell them who he is. That's the whole point." He looked at Dan again. "Could I wait for him up there at the pass? I mean, I could camp out there and I'd know what he looks like."

"Technically, camping isn't allowed in the Sonora Pass parking lot," Dan said. "I can't tell you that's okay. But we kind of give the trail angels a break there. They usually have people at the pass all the time. You could probably hang out with them…"

Travis nodded, his mouth slightly open, waiting for Dan to continue.

"Or you could day-hike south out of the pass each day and plan to meet him somewhere on the trail before he arrives at the pass. If he's really taken a vow of silence, it might be easier for you to explain what you want to do that way, instead of trying to do it in the mix of other hikers and the rest of the angels at Sonora Pass…"

"Yeah, I could do that!" Travis exclaimed. "I've hiked that trail before. I could even take a few snacks or drinks or something for him. And then we could get it all settled before he gets to the trailhead."

Dan agreed. "But you probably need to be prepared for the possibility that he won't want your help and may not even want to listen to you… I mean, you need to be respectful of what he is doing, and how he is choosing to hike the trail."

"Oh, totally," Travis agreed, nodding vigorously. "But he will need to re-supply, even I know that, and all I want to do is offer him a ride into town. I just want to be part of it, if I can."

Dan thought his over. "Okay. You don't need a permit for a day hike, and as long as you stay with the trail angel group when you are not hiking, I don't think there's a problem. We just had a meeting about this today, and you know Cal Healey, the sheriff?"

Travis nodded.

"Cal is going to be the primary LEO up there. Make sure you say hello to him, so that he knows it's you."

"Got it," Travis said. "Thank you so much!" He turned and started for the door.

"Travis! Wait!" Doris called out. "Give me a hug." As the two embraced, Dan could hear her say, "You be careful up there and stay safe."

"Thanks, Grandma, I will," Travis replied, sounding just a bit exasperated.

And he was gone out the door.

chapter 3

By the end of the day, most of the email blizzard had slowed down to a few small flurries, and Dan began to feel as if he could begin to focus on the rest of his job. He liked to get things off his desk and out of his inbox before he left for the day, and it looked like he was going to achieve that.

He certainly had time to read a text message from Kristen, suggesting that maybe they could do dinner on Thursday night, this time at her house. He answered that one right away, and it made the rest of the afternoon fly by.

Doris liked to say that he was afraid to leave anything for the following morning. She was the one to keep an eye on the clock and suggest to him that it was time to go home, even if a few things were hanging around late in the day.

That included an email from Bruce Spielman. Bruce had been married to Dan's sister Diane but they had divorced quite a few years ago. The mail was simple. He just wanted to give Dan a call to chat about something that had come up. As with all the other emails, Dan sent a quick note back, assuring Bruce that he'd be happy to talk, and giving Bruce the number for his landline. No need to give him the cell number.

And then he turned off his computer.

When the phone rang right at five o'clock, Doris deliberated whether she should even answer it or not. And when she did, she gave Dan a roll of her eyes to let him know she'd made the wrong decision.

"I think he's already left for the day," Dan heard her say.

He wandered out of his office and motioned to ask her who it was. She wrote a quick note on a piece of paper. "Gina from SRC."

Dan gave a sigh and pointed to himself, nodding slightly as he did so.

"Oh, wait, Gina," Doris said. "I see him now. Hang on a sec."

Doris put the call on hold and handed him the phone.

"This sounds like a long one," she said.

Dan grinned and punched the phone button. "Hi, Gina. What's up?"

"Hi, Dan. How are you?" Gina asked. Dan knew this was going to be a problem, because when Gina asks how you are doing, it means you are not going to be doing quite so well by the time you are done talking to her. But her work at the Sierra Research Center was important, and Dan and the rest of the local USFS staff tried to be as supportive as possible.

"I'm good," Dan said quickly. "What's up?"

"Well, I think we have a problem," Gina said. And then she waited.

"Okay," Dan gave in. "What's the problem?"

"I probably should have waited until tomorrow for this," Gina continued. "But we were so upset that I thought it would be better to let you know right away."

Dan gave a sigh. In a quieter voice, he said, "So what's going on?"

"You know how we're doing that survey of the Belding ground squirrels?" she asked.

Dan nodded, knowing that she couldn't see this over the phone. Also knowing that she wouldn't care one way or the other.

"Well, one of our researchers got chased out of one of the canyons above Summit Creek."

She paused.

"What do you mean, chased out of there?" Dan asked. "By a bear? By people? Not by a squirrel…"

"Very funny," Gina said. But she was not amused. "By a guy with a gun and a dog."

"What?" Dan had a hard time believing it. "What do you mean?"

"She is really shaken up, Dan." Gina was now beginning to get emotional, and Dan could hear it in her voice. He looked at Doris, who was waiting for the call to end. Dan motioned her to go ahead and leave. She didn't move.

"She was hiking down Summit Creek, exploring all of the side canyons," Gina continued. "When she started up this canyon, all of a sudden there was a huge dog in front of her, acting very territorial and aggressive. And while she tried to calm him down, a guy showed up with a rifle and told her to get the hell out of there."

Dan searched his memory to see if he could picture the place. "So, was this up on the way to Iceland Lake and Granite Dome?"

"No, no," Gina said. "Further up the creek, and on the north side of the valley, past Sheep Camp."

Dan had only been up there once, on the way to Brown Bear Pass, and he wasn't sure he remembered the terrain very well. "So that's it?" he asked. "The guy just chased her out of there?"

Gina gave a gasp. "Well, she wasn't about to argue with a guy pointing a rifle at her," she said. "This is one of our summer interns. She's a good kid, and frankly, I think she probably could have dealt with the dog—she's great with animals. But an asshole with a rifle is a different story."

"Yeah, no kidding," Dan agreed. "So did he say anything else to her? I mean, what exactly did this guy say and do?"

Gina paused a moment to compose herself. "First he told the dog to sit. Which it didn't do. That made her nervous right away, like he didn't really have control over the dog. Then he told her that she couldn't come up into that part of the canyon. He told her it was closed."

"That's crazy," Dan said. "It's not closed."

"I know, but that's what he told Annie. Anyway, Annie just explained that she was doing research on the ground squirrels and needed to include the area in her survey. That's when he told her that his dog had chased all the squirrels out of there anyway, or eaten them."

"Oh, Jesus," Dan sighed. "I don't suppose that this guy gave her his name, or any reason?'

"Oh, he did," Gina replied. "And you are going to love it. He told her that the area was closed because it was a mining operation, and nobody was allowed in that area because it was closed to the public. That's when he showed her his rifle, just in case she hadn't noticed that he was holding it up in front of himself."

"Crap," Dan muttered into the phone. He glanced at Doris. Her face was grim, lips set firmly against each other. Even though she couldn't hear the call, she knew this wasn't good.

"So are you ready?" Gina asked. "Annie was smart enough to punch in her GPS coordinates, so I can tell you exactly where this is."

"Yeah," Dan replied, reaching for a pencil. Doris handed him a yellow legal pad to write on.

With the coordinates written down, Dan continued with Gina. "There's nothing we can do about this today, obviously, but I'll check in with Steve Matson. I'm sure he'll want to get on this right away. Is Annie okay?"

"She's okay," Gina told him. "She's pretty shaken up, but she's also had time to hike out of there. And that gave her time to get really angry. Right now I wouldn't bet on that dog if they were in a fight."

Dan chuckled. "Sorry, I'm not making light of this," he explained. "But I think I'd like to meet Annie."

"She's a great kid," Gina told him. "But right now, I think we're going to keep her close to the office for a few days."

"Sounds like a good idea," Dan said. "Does she have a physical description of this guy?" he asked.

"I can have you talk to her whenever you want," Gina was quick to answer. "I sent her home to give her some time tonight to get cleaned up and get herself pulled together, but I can have her meet you at the office tomorrow morning when you start, if you want."

"That would be great," Dan said.

Doris waited expectantly as Dan hung up the phone, her eyes riveted on his.

Dan sighed and explained, "Some wacko up by Brown Bear Pass chased one of Gina's researchers out."

"Oh my," Doris' eyes got even bigger. "Was she hurt?"

Dan shook his head. He looked at the map again, this time carefully plugging in the GPS coordinates while Doris peered at the map from the other side. It was going to be most of a day's hike just to get there. Dan sighed again.

"So what happened?" she asked Dan.

"Apparently, someone has decided to start mining up there."

"In the middle of the wilderness?" Doris was aghast.

"In the middle of the wilderness," Dan nodded.

He worked through the next steps in his mind: Call Steve Matson and find out whom Steve could assign to a trip up there. Call the Sheriff's office to let them know about the situation and see if they could help. Call the other USFS offices in the area and let them know that there was a problem. Steve would decide if they had to stop issuing permits for anyone in that area. And that would be a mess, because this was only a few miles from the PCT.

Dan looked up to see Doris opening the folder of wilderness permits.

"Well," she said, "Maybe he didn't get a permit, but if he did, maybe we can figure out who he is…"

Dan glanced at the clock, which now read something well after closing hours. "You don't have to do that," Dan said. "Go home. I'll take this over to the Pizza Oven and look through these while I eat."

"Are you buying?" Doris asked with a smile.

Dan laughed. "Yeah, okay, sure. I'm buying."

"Let's go!" Doris gently pushed Dan towards the door.

chapter 4

When the waitress left the table, Doris leaned over to Dan and whispered, "You know she's interested in you, don't you?"

Dan was furious to find himself blushing. "Come on, Doris, she's just being friendly because she wants a good tip. Besides, she must be at least ten years younger than me."

Doris fixed him with a glare. "You are clueless," she said. "But it's nice that you are seeing Kristen." She smiled. "And apparently not interested in anyone else."

It was time to change the subject. Dan pulled out the folder of permits and opened it up. He took a guess and handed Doris about half of the permits from the top. "Anybody who is going to Brown Bear Pass, or Emigrant Meadows Lake…"

Doris nodded. "Do we know how many people?"

Dan shook his head. "But my guess is it's probably someone in for more than a few days. That might be our first clue."

By the time the pizza had arrived, Dan was thankful that they had asked for a larger table. Papers were in stacks spread out over most of the available space. The waitress put the pizza down on the edge of the table, gave them two plates, and asked if there was anything else they needed. Dan shook his head without really looking up, studying a permit that was almost illegible.

"Her name is Mandy," Doris said to Dan.

Dan glanced up and gave a chuckle. "Good to know. Thank you."

"She's new. I don't know her," Doris continued.

"Okay," Dan changed the subject. "Here's one. Three people going to spend a week up by Upper Emigrant Lake."

Doris sighed and picked up a piece of her half of the pizza—the side without mushrooms. She took a bite, then took the permit paper from Dan and dropped it into a small pile in the middle of the table.

Dan absentmindedly took a piece of pizza.

"Mmmph!" Doris grunted with her mouth full. Dan looked up. Doris pointed to the mushroom side of the pizza. "Hats fer hoo," she said. "Hisses my," she continued, pointing to her side of the pie.

Dan put the piece of pizza back and picked up a slice with mushrooms and took a bite, eyes back on the paperwork in front of him.

Doris swallowed and cleared her throat. "You know, if he really is trying to mine up there, then he'll have to stay up there for more than a few days," she said. "And if he is serious—and he sounds pretty serious, with a gun and all that—then he'll be up there for quite a while."

Dan got her point. "So either he comes out every week to clean up and re-supply, or he gets someone to pack in more supplies to him."

Doris immediately started flipping through the permit applications, looking for those that had been faxed in by the local packing outfits. As she found them, she started passing them to Dan.

The first three were for trips into Bucks Lakes, probably for fishing trips. Then she picked one up and started reading to Dan.

"Overnight trip to Summit Creek to drop off supplies." She looked up. "This one is out of Kennedy Meadows." She handed it to

Dan.

Dan read the name on the trip, one of the regular packers for Kennedy Meadows. "Okay, so this might be the re-supply trip." He checked the dates. "And it was ten… eleven days ago. But that means there must be an earlier trip to take him in there to begin with…"

Doris was quickly thumbing through the papers in her stack. Then she looked up. "These stop about three weeks ago. It must be in your stack."

Dan put his pizza down so that he could use both hands, quickly getting a spot of grease on the first permit he touched.

Doris handed him a napkin.

He grabbed it and kept thumbing through the permits.

"Got it," he said. "June 29th. Man, that is early for up there. In a normal year he would have been up to his armpits in snow… They would have been," he corrected. "Two people. Leader's name is Cameron Scott from Modesto…"

"You think that's it?" Doris asked.

"Sure looks like it," Dan said. "Going in for two weeks… but no real itinerary. Camping in Summit Creek Canyon for two weeks? Who does that?"

Doris gave him a half-nod of assent. "Does that name ring a bell with you?" she asked.

Dan shook his head. He was reading the form to see if he could get any more information. When he looked up at Doris, he saw that she had pulled out her phone. "What?"

"Not much here, from what I can see. It's an unusual name, so I thought I'd do a quick check. Looks like he's a big fan of the State of Jefferson," she added. "But nothing about mining."

Dan laughed. "Not surprising. I don't think people who mine

for gold are in the habit of telling other people about it…"

Doris looked serious. "This guy is a bit of a wacko," she said. "He's got some links to some very ugly websites here…" She handed the phone to Dan.

The website she showed him had photos of armed men raising their guns in front of a banner that said "GOVT OUT of local lands," and another that said, "Don't tread on me," with an image of a rattlesnake holding an assault weapon.

"Great," Dan said. "Just what we need up here." He handed the phone back to Doris, his mind working through the ramifications of what he now knew.

"I don't like this a bit," Doris said. "Thank God you can turn this over to the Sheriff's office."

"Yeah," Dan agreed.

Doris picked up a new slice of pizza, took a bite, and grimaced. "Pizza's cold."

Dan grunted, his mind elsewhere. He took a bite and chewed thoughtfully.

When Mandy finally returned with their bill, Doris didn't bother to speak about it. She watched Dan leave cash on the table, which included a hefty tip, and they walked out into the mountain air.

"At least you left a nice tip for her," Doris said.

Dan gave her a thin smile. "See you in the morning."

Doris nodded and patted his arm. "Goodnight, Dan."

Dan watched her get into her SUV and drive off. He was grateful that he wasn't going to be responsible for this mess.

That was Steve Matson's job.

chapter 5

When Dan arrived at his house later that night, there was a phone message on his home phone from Bruce Spielman. Dan had forgotten all about his email.

Dan listened to the message. Bruce sounded positively apologetic about calling him, hoped it wasn't too much of an imposition. Asked Dan to call him back ASAP, if that was possible, and left a number. And Bruce asked him to call no matter how late he got in.

Dan wondered if something was wrong with his sister and considered giving Diane a call. But Bruce hadn't mentioned her in his email or his phone message. And while Dan had often found that Bruce had a slight tendency to arrogance, neither communication gave any indication of that. Maybe Bruce had mellowed over the years.

He dialed Bruce's number and was surprised to hear Bruce answer on the first ring.

"Dan Courtwright!" Bruce greeted him. "How are you?"

There was just a bit too much stress on the second question for Dan's taste. It sounded like Bruce was making every effort to be friendly—something that made Dan's antenna go into full alert.

Dan assured him he was fine and volleyed back a question about Bruce.

"Doing great," Bruce responded. "Really great. Trying to keep busy and all…"

Dan waited for a moment, thinking Bruce would take the lead in the conversation, but he didn't. So Dan asked about Casey, his niece.

"Oh, she's great," Bruce replied. "I've even been helping out a bit with her softball team."

Dan granted that this was a good thing. Last he had heard, Bruce had fallen behind on his child support payments, and was not playing a role in his daughter's life. It was a topic of conversation every time Dan talked to his sister Diane—which wasn't all that often these days.

Dan's patience ran out and he asked Bruce, "So what's up, Bruce?"

Bruce gave a long sigh.

"I really hate to bother you with this, but I don't know who else to call, Dan. And there might be something in this for you."

Dan hoped with all his heart that he wasn't going to be asked to serve as an intermediary between Bruce and Diane.

"But it's kind of a long story," Bruce continued. "I mean, to make it short…" Bruce paused here.

Dan waited.

"Well, I guess the easiest way to explain it is that a guy I know owes me some money, see?" Bruce began. "And he doesn't really have any money at all. So I asked what else he had that he could use to cover the bet."

Dan rolled his eyes at that one.

"I mean, to cover his debt," Bruce corrected himself. "Like I said, he owed me some money."

Dan remembered that one of the issues in the divorce had been

Bruce's less than careful approach to money.

"So I asked him, 'What have you got instead?'" Bruce soldiered on with his story. "And the next thing you know, he's talking about this mining claim."

Dan chuckled. "That should keep you busy," he said.

"Well, I don't know if it's worth anything," Bruce said. "But it's all the guy had, so I took it. I figured that something is better than nothing, right?"

Dan chuckled again. "Yeah, but only if the mining claim is worth something…"

"So that's why I am calling you, Dan," Bruce jumped in. "I think you might know something about this."

Dan shook his head as he answered. "I don't know much about mining, Bruce. I never really got the bug, and all I really know is that these days it's a lot harder to get permits to do any kind of mining at all."

"Yeah, I know that," Bruce answered. "I understand that. But the reason I was calling you is that this one is up by you. It's right where Wildcat Creek runs into the Stanislaus River."

Dan thought for a minute. "That's very rugged country down there," he told Bruce. "I don't know many people who have been down in that canyon."

"I know that, too," Bruce said. "But the guy said he knows a way to get in there."

Dan let out a long breath of air. "Oh, there are ways to get there, but it isn't going to be easy. And there's no way to get any equipment at all in there, not without building a road." He let this sink in. "And a road would be unbelievably expensive, even if you could get a permit to build it. Which you won't."

"Yeah, yeah, I know," Bruce replied. "I'm not looking at that.

It's a placer claim. There's a section right where the creek meets the river that's pure bedrock. And that's where the gold is."

Dan thought this over. "So what are you thinking?" he asked. "Are you just going to hike in there and start panning for gold?"

"Well, that's what I wanted to talk to you about, Dan. I'd like to get in there and try that, to see what kind of gold I might find."

Dan smiled at this. "You do know that just about every river, creek and tributary in this whole state has already been panned over and over again in the last hundred and fifty years, don't you?"

"Oh sure, I know, but this one is so remote, I figure there's a chance that it's still got some areas that haven't been worked for a long time. And maybe that means there will still be some gold for me to find."

"I'll make you a bet," Dan offered. "I'll bet when you get down there, you'll find stacks of river rocks on the banks, where the miners left their tailings back in the day."

"Yeah, I know," Bruce answered. Dan couldn't help thinking that Bruce seemed to know everything, but was still calling Dan for help. "But I still think there might be something down there."

"Well, I wish you luck," Dan said.

"Thanks for that," Bruce replied. "Any miner will take all the luck he can get. But that's not really why I called."

With another pause, Dan finally gave in and asked the question. "Okay, why did you call?"

"You don't have to give me an answer right away," Bruce said. "Take a few days to think it over. But I'd like to invite you to be part of this. You don't need to do any of the work unless you want to, but I'd love to be able to consult with you on this. How does ten percent sound?"

Dan laughed quietly. "Yeah...I don't think so, Bruce. I

appreciate the offer, but I've seen too many guys up here spend too much of their lives looking for gold without finding much."

"Look, Dan, there's no risk for you," Bruce answered. "I'm not asking you to invest. I just want to be able to give you a call from time to time and get your sense of things."

"My sense of things is that this is a waste of your time, Bruce," Dan said. "Even if there is some gold in there, by the time you add up the hours it will take you to get in there and work the area, my best 'sense of things' is that you would be better off to spend the same amount of time working at a fast food joint for minimum wage."

This time it was Bruce who laughed. "Yeah, but this is a lot more fun, Dan."

"If you like digging in mud, living in the water, and working your ass off," Dan offered.

"All part of the adventure, along with the possibility of finding a nugget or two that would really pay off," Bruce said.

"Which is a very, very tiny possibility," Dan said.

Bruce laughed again. "We'll see, Dan. I'll still keep you posted. And the offer is still good. Ten percent of any gold I find. All you have to do is give me advice when I ask for it."

Dan laughed. "I just gave you the best advice I could."

"Yeah, so okay, you're in for ten percent," Bruce said. "The good part about this deal is that you can give me advice, and I don't have to take it."

"Okay," Dan agreed. "But I don't need the ten percent. Thanks anyway."

"Look," Bruce said. "If you're right and I don't make any money on this deal, your ten percent isn't important. And if I do really make some dough, it won't hurt to give you ten percent."

A thought suddenly occurred to Dan. He could give any money in the deal to his niece, maybe for college.

"That's a deal, Bruce," he said. "I'll give you advice, you won't take it, and you give me ten percent of any gold you find."

Dan was happy to agree to the deal, and Bruce promised to head into the canyon in the next couple of days. For a moment, Dan was worried that Bruce might ask to use Dan's house as a basecamp as part of the deal, but Bruce didn't ask.

And Dan didn't offer.

chapter 6

Dan ended the call with Bruce and was startled by his cell phone ringing almost immediately. It was Steve Matson.

The conversation with Steve Matson did not go the way Dan had envisioned it. The Sheriff's Department had a major mess on their hands, with a dead body found in an abandoned mine shaft. They were stretched a little too thin to give much help, at least today. And one of Dan's colleagues had a knee problem. And then there was the situation up at Sonora Pass and all the PCT hikers. The more Dan talked to Steve, the more it became clear that there was only one person who could hike up to Summit Creek and find out what the hell was going on up there.

Steve did promise some help. He would meet with Annie and debrief her about the whole incident and pass that information on to Dan. He would also call the FBI about Cameron Scott and see what they knew, and if they could help. All of that would happen first thing in the morning.

But meanwhile, Steve was very concerned that hikers might wander up into that area and somebody would get hurt. And he wanted to make sure that didn't happen. The first step would be to close the Summit Creek trail at both ends and then station someone up there to make sure of two things:

1. That no hikers bypassed the closure signs and hiked into

Summit Creek.

2. That Cameron Scott and whoever might be with him were monitored to make sure that we knew where they were and what they were doing.

What was needed was someone to head up there first thing tomorrow morning and serve as the first recon on the situation.

And that person was Dan.

"Take your radio, and keep your head down up there," Steve said. "I don't want you to solve this. I just need you to make sure that nobody else does anything stupid up there."

Dan sighed. It was not the way he wanted to spend his next couple of days, and it was certainly not why he had joined the USFS. Steve heard the sigh.

"Dan, I am dead serious," he stressed. "This is not your problem to solve. Just go up there and keep everyone else away until we can get the right team to engage these guys."

"Okay," Dan agreed.

"And take your radio," Steve continued, "and make sure it's charged." He was aware that Dan was known for not always following that advice. "I'll need to be able to reach you, and I'll need you to be able to tell me what's going on. I'll let you know as soon as I know anything more, from this kid Annie or the Sheriff or anyone."

"Got it," Dan replied.

"One more thing," Matson continued. "This is all about you being safe and making sure everyone else is safe."

Dan hung up the phone and looked at his backpack. It was more or less ready to go, except for the food.

He checked the cabinet next to the fridge and found plenty of packets of instant oatmeal and cocoa. Dan thought about it and figured that three days was enough. If he had to stay any longer than that, he would ask someone to bring him more food. Lots of dried fruit, so he took three different flavors. He only had two freeze-dried dinners: a Beef Stroganoff and Chili Mac and Cheese. Dan grabbed two packets of ramen and added them in. In his fridge he had half a hard salami and some Romano cheese. He added in a box of Cheez-its and started packing his bear canister. He managed to make it fit, even though the Cheez-its were probably sawdust by the time the lid was tight.

He repacked the pack with the food and closed it all up. There was probably something he was missing, but he couldn't think what it was. He remembered that he would have to print out a few signs that he could post on the trail. He thought about making a list and then decided that sleep was more important. He headed for bed and set his alarm for 5 a.m. His phone told him that the alarm would ring in six hours and fifteen minutes.

Dan flopped into bed and closed his eyes. As he fell asleep, a thought passed through his brain. It had turned out that this was not really Steve Matson's problem after all.

It was just showing a dim glow of light in the east when Dan's alarm sounded. He raced through his morning ritual, wolfing down a bowl of granola, taking a quick hot shower, and throwing on his clothes and pulling on his socks while his toes were still not completely dry from the shower. He ran a comb quickly through his hair, laced up his boots, and grabbed the backpack.

He climbed into his truck and started driving up to the ranger station. He was halfway there when he remembered that the TP in his pack was dangerously low. He would have to pick up a resupply from the restroom there. Not ideal, but it would work.

At the ranger station he flicked on his computer and the printer and printed out a few signs for the trail. He was able to use a previous file and just change some of the text, so that went quickly. He printed out six (he could only think of three or four places to put a sign, but it never hurt to have a few more) and grabbed a similar number of plastic sleeves, along with a roll of tape and a staple gun.

As he opened up his pack, he remembered the TP. In the supply closet there was the remains of a package of twelve rolls with only three left. He took two rolls out, leaving them on the stack, and wrapped the remaining roll in the plastic of the packaging. It was more than he needed, but he liked the idea of the extra plastic. It could always come in handy on the trail.

Dan closed up his pack, locked up the office, tossed the pack into his truck and drove up to Kennedy Meadows. He noticed that now he didn't need his headlights anymore.

chapter 7

By the time Dan reached the trailhead the sun was out in force, and it was a beautiful day for a hike. He parked his truck in the trailhead parking lot and hoisted on his pack. With the staple gun, the radio, and extra batteries, it was at least a couple of pounds heavier than usual, and he knew he'd feel it on the climb up to Relief Reservoir.

He posted the first notice on the trailhead sign in the parking lot itself, then hiked down to Kennedy Meadows to tell them what was going on.

He spotted Randy Fuller in the stable and stopped in to chat with him. Randy had worked there for what seemed like ages, and Dan always liked his ready smile and dry humor.

Randy remembered the two guys that were camping up in Summit Creek. "I took them up there about a month ago," he told Dan. "They said they were doing some kind of geology research. And we're supposed to take them another resupply in a couple of days."

Dan nodded. "We may have to reschedule that one," Dan said. "I'm headed up there right now, and I'll let you know what the story is. Right now, we're closing access up there until we know exactly what's going on."

"They took a good load of stuff up there," Randy explained.

"I think we ended up with seven mules on that trip. And they each carried a pretty good pack, too."

Dan asked Randy if he'd seen any weapons.

Randy snorted. "When I pack a mule, I know what's in every single bag. That's the only way I can balance out the loads and make it all work. When I told those guys about that, they immediately grabbed a few things and agreed to carry them up in their packs. I don't know what kind of guns they had, but they had a couple of rifle cases, and I assume there were guns inside them."

Dan grunted his agreement. "Thanks."

Randy waited to see if Dan had anything else to ask. When he didn't get another question, he turned to walk back to the horses. When he had taken a few steps he stopped and turned back to Dan. "So, if those guys call in and ask for their re-supply, what do I tell them?"

"Just tell them that the Forest Service has closed that area to traffic for a while," Dan said. "But my guess is that I am going to run into them before they call you. And I'll tell them that myself."

Randy thought this over. "Okay. Be careful up there," he said. "Those guys seemed harmless enough, but they might be wound a little tighter than they need to be."

"Thanks," Dan said, adding a wry smile. "Just what I wanted to hear."

Randy laughed and turned away quickly to talk to one of his mules that was acting up. Dan turned up the trail and started the long walk up to Summit Creek. It was already warm in the sun, and Dan knew that it was going to be a long, hot hike. There were a few people fishing in the river above Kennedy Meadows, but by the time the trail started to climb up towards Relief Reservoir Dan was alone.

At the junction with the Kennedy Creek trail, Dan stopped and posted another note about the closure. He was just about to start up the trail again when his radio squawked at him. Steve Matson had some news.

"I spoke to the young lady Annie this morning," He said. "She gave me a pretty good description of the guy who confronted her. Maybe a bit under six feet, medium build, mid-forties or fifty. He has a beard, but it's trimmed. He was wearing a plaid shirt and jeans. And a ball cap. And he had what she called an assault rifle—something that looked military to her. And a big dog. She said it was bigger and meatier than a pit bull. And very aggressive."

Great, Dan thought. That should be fun.

Dan heard Steve back on the radio. "Just remember that your job is to make sure nobody gets hurt up there," he heard Steve saying. "We are sending back-up for you, but it looks like that may not happen today. Maybe not until tomorrow."

Dan told him about the conversation with Randy.

"Yeah," Steve replied. "And Doris told me what she found out about this guy on his website this morning. Sounds like a bit of a wacko."

Dan thought this over. "I am just going to try to hike up to Brown Bear Pass and post a notice up there, and then I'll come back down and set up camp below where these guys are supposed to be, according to Annie. And I'll wait to hear from you."

"Thanks, Dan," Steve answered. "That's the plan. And stay safe, please."

"That's exactly what I plan to do," Dan agreed.

The trail now began a steady climb up above the reservoir, slowly following the creek and then switch-backing up to Lunch Meadow. The last time Dan had hiked this trail it was to leave the trail about here and head west to hike cross-country to the granite-bound lakes above. It had been a wonderful trip, and he had only seen three people in four days.

If he was lucky, that would be true today, too. But this time he noticed that the sparkling creek was carrying a hefty load of silt. A nasty gnawing in his stomach made him slow down for a minute to stare at the creek. No question about it. It looked like thinned paint, instead of the gin-clear water it should be. Dan was beginning to develop a healthy dislike of this particular job.

Once above the meadow he posted more notices on the signs there marking the trail to Lower Emigrant Lake, and decided it was well past lunch time. For the first time, he made the connection with the name of the meadow, and smiled. For a fast hiker like Dan, Lunch Meadow was right where it ought to be.

He took off his pack and immediately felt the cool wash of air over the back of his shirt, which was saturated with sweat. He found a flat rock and opened up his pack. His lunch, some crackers, cheese and dried fruit, was right on top where he could get it easily. And he broke out the last bottle of his water. He figured it would be easier to filter the creek above where these clowns were mining. That way, he wouldn't have to pre-filter everything through his bandanna.

Dan eased himself further back on the rock and felt the sun warm on his face. He chewed slowly, taking a sip of water with each bite to help wash down the dry crackers. Across the valley a raven slowly flew along the top of the ridge, then settled into the branches of a tree. Other than a gentle puff of wind from time to time, it was absolutely silent. Dan was making more noise chewing his crackers than the rest of the natural world combined.

From where he sat it was another three miles to the next trail junction at Emigrant Meadow Lake. He could step that off in a little more than an hour, without pushing it. Which meant he could be back here by about three or maybe four in the afternoon. Plenty hours of sunlight left to set up camp. And maybe poke around and see what he might find.

He remembered Steve's warning. But he also had all afternoon. Once the notices were posted, he could decide his next steps.

Dan ate a fresh apple, a treat he always allowed himself on the first day on the trail. And he didn't worry about carrying out any trash. He ate the whole apple, core and all, and tossed the stem away in the brush by the creek. After nibbling a few peanut M&Ms for dessert he pulled out his day pack, loaded it up with what he would need in the next couple of hours, including the water filter, and looked for a good place to stash his main pack.

He tucked it behind a couple of boulders at the base of a grove of juniper trees, with the bear canister thirty yards away. It looked fine: slightly hidden from the trail, but not hard to find. When he got back down to the trail, he looked back to see, but from there it was well hidden by the rocks. He picked up his day pack and started up the trail again.

From the GPS coordinates, he was getting pretty darn close to where Annie had run into trouble. Dan studiously stayed on the trail as he hiked, but his eyes scanned the slopes above him, looking for any sign of the mine or its crew. It seemed to him that there would probably be a very faint use trail along one of the side creeks, right near Annie's coordinates.

Dan stopped to look for a few seconds, but that was not his problem, at least not today. Today his only job was to put up the notices along the trail, and then turn anyone else away from the area. He forced himself to keep walking up the canyon, eyes more or less straight ahead.

As he moved up the trail, he wondered if he was being

watched—wondered if he was being watched through the scope of a rifle.

Once at the junction, Dan posted the notices. From near the lake he could faintly hear voices, and he decided to go check them out.

It looked like a group of six or seven young people, resting down by the water. They had their packs off and it looked like they might be done for the day, but Dan didn't see any tents up.

He called out to the group, realizing that some of them might be skinny dipping in the lake. It was always a good idea to give people a little advance warning, he knew.

"Hi, guys!" he called out.

The response was not exactly enthusiastic, but at least a couple of the kids responded.

"Just stopping in to tell you that we have a bit of a problem on the trail back through Summit Creek," Dan said. "Are you headed that way?"

One of the kids seemed slightly more in charge. He was wearing shorts and a cowboy hat and eating a fistful of something Dan could not identify. "Not until tomorrow," the young man said. "We're heading out tomorrow through Kennedy Meadows."

Dan nodded. "Yeah, I'm afraid you'll have to go back to Lower Emigrant and take that trail out tomorrow," he said.

"What?" Now all of the group began to gather around Dan. "What's the problem? We can always just climb around anything in the way."

Dan shook his head. "I'm sorry, the trail is closed. There is a real safety issue, and we can't let anyone use that trail until it is resolved. And that won't happen today, or maybe even tomorrow."

Dan knew the look that worked its way around the group of

young hikers. They appreciated his concern, but they were pretty sure they could get through anyway.

"And I'll be camped right in the middle of that until we get the problem cleared up," he added. "Are you planning on hiking out tomorrow?"

"Yeah," one of the girls in the group admitted.

"Okay," Dan nodded. "If you are worried about the long day tomorrow, I'd really suggest that you hike back to Lower Emigrant Lake and camp there. That will give you a shorter hike tomorrow. And that trail is open and clear."

He heard some grumbling about backtracking.

"What exactly is the problem?" one of the girls asked.

"We're not sure," Dan said. "But we have reports of someone who is armed and threatening people along that section of the trail. I just came through there, and didn't see anyone, but until we can be sure, we can't let anyone down there."

"Jesus!" a young guy with a small goatee and ball cap on said. "What an asshole."

Dan sighed. "So, do me a favor and go back around on the other trail?" He ended that with a question.

Most of kids agreed in one way or another, and just then Dan noticed one of the girls picking up a speck of micro-trash and putting it into her pocket.

"And thanks for that," he said, nodding at the girl. "It's amazing how much little bits like that get left around."

This was all it took for the whole group to assure him that they were really careful about trash and were model citizens in general.

Dan smiled. "Thanks, guys. I'm camped right down below in the valley. If anything changes, I'll come and find you and let you know."

chapter 8

Dan took his time hiking back up to the pass. From the top of the pass, he could see a long way down into Summit Creek Canyon. He stopped there to spend a few minutes just watching the canyon. There was little life to see. Behind him he was happy to see the kids packed up and walking back down the trail to Lower Emigrant Lake. That was one problem avoided.

Off in the distance he could see the peaks he knew, and he clicked them off in his mind. He took a glance over toward Lost Lake, knowing it was out of sight around the ridge. When Dan had first come to work in the Stanislaus, he didn't have a strong connection with either the office or the wilderness. But that had changed. After four years of walking these trails, this now felt like home.

Dan remembered a conversation he'd had with Kristen a few weeks ago. She asked him if he felt a sense of ownership of this part of the Sierra. She had a way of asking him big questions like that, questions that really made him stop and think.

As he thought about it, he realized that the answer was yes—but not in the way she might think. He didn't feel as if he owned the mountains. It was more a case of the mountains owning him. It took him a while to explain it, and he wasn't sure if he really did explain it very well. The way he saw it, the mountains were in charge, and his job was to make sure they were happy. Dan smiled when he remembered that Kristen really seemed to like that answer.

He was never quite sure what Kristen liked about him, but he had stored that one away for the future. She had liked that one.

Still smiling, Dan took out his binoculars to scan the canyon below. It looked sleepy in the late afternoon light, and Dan calculated that if he headed down right now, he might just be able to enjoy a short nap in the sun before dinner.

Something on the hillside below caught his attention. A glint of the sun off something that was not natural. Dan honed in on it, and muttered. Behind one of the rocks right up where Annie had been confronted, Dan could see something metallic. Crap! It looked like a solar panel.

No wonder they had noticed Annie before she got up into their side canyon. These guys had some kind of equipment set-up down there, maybe cameras or motion sensors.

In addition to the big dog.

He took a deep breath, put on his daypack, and started hiking back down into Summit Creek Canyon. All the while he watched the side canyon. But by the time he was back at his pack, he had seen nothing unusual. From where he had planned to set up camp, even the solar panel was hidden behind a rock and a couple of bushes. He debated getting on the radio to tell Steve Matson what he had learned, but there was time enough for that later. He wanted to set up his tent while there was plenty of light.

It didn't take him long. One of the things Dan enjoyed was being efficient in the back country. He liked the idea of minimal equipment, well-maintained and easy to use. The tent was up, his pad inflated, and his sleeping bag laid out in less than ten minutes. He put his bear can up between two rocks, straightened up his pack, took off his boots, and put on his camp sandals. Everything was set.

Dan sat down for a few minutes and considered that nap again. Then he remembered the water. He picked up his filter and water bottles, and slowly walked upstream to where the water was running clear and clean. He could see now how obviously the side canyon was bringing down silty water into the main creek. Dan stopped at the confluence to study it, then found a nice rock where he could sit and pump his filter. The creek burbled happily, and the rhythmic action of his pumping added its voice to the soundscape. A few tiny trout raced into the darkness under a rock. Dan watched to make sure that his intake tube was completely under the water in the tiny pool he had selected. Falling into a steady rhythm, he began to pump away.

And that's when the hairs on his neck suddenly stood up.

Somebody was behind him. He was sure of it. Trying not to look startled, Dan slowly turned around. Thirty feet away was a guy in jeans and plaid shirt carrying a rifle. And next to him was a very large dog. It looked something like a mix between a large boxer and a huge pit bull. Not a dog you would want to mess with. Over the sound of the stream, Dan could hear the very low but serious growl of warning from the dog.

Dan nodded, without saying anything. He felt at a huge disadvantage, squatting on a slick rock down near the stream, while the man and dog towered over him.

"You looking for me?" the guy asked him.

Dan shrugged. "I don't know. Should I be? Who are you?"

The man ignored Dan's questions. "I knew that little bitch would complain to somebody," he said.

Dan smiled a tight smile. "What are you doing up here?" he asked.

The man stared at Dan. "That's none of your business."

Dan's smile stayed on his face. "Actually, since I'm a ranger in charge of this area, anything that happens here is my business. That's what I get paid to do."

The man seemed unconvinced. "I'm completely legal," he said.

Dan nodded. "Okay. Legal for what?"

"I filed a claim, and it is registered totally legal."

"A mining claim?" Dan asked.

The man didn't respond.

Dan let him wait for a while, then added. "You know, the claim only reserved the site for your use. You still need an approved EIR, and a use permit. . . You need a lot more than just the claim to actually start mining."

The man slipped his rifle off his shoulder and held it in his hands. Dan did not like the change. "Just saying—that's the way it works," he explained.

Dan could see the guy's fingers moving around on the rifle. Twitching, almost.

"What are you going to do about it?" the guy asked Dan. It was both a question and a challenge.

Dan snorted quietly. "That's not my decision," he said. "That's one that gets made way above my pay scale, somewhere between the Forest Headquarters and Washington DC." He hoped that answer would calm the situation down. "And by the way, the Forest Service has closed this entire area. Nobody in or out. Trailhead is closed."

He could see the man was thinking this over. Meanwhile, the dog seemed to be just a tiny bit less aggressive.

Dan waited.

The man looked up the hill at Dan's camp. "You camping here tonight?"

Dan nodded. "Yep. That's my tent over there."

The man stared at Dan. "I'm gonna give you some advice," he said. "I'd advise you to stay on that side of the creek here. You never know about Duke here. He tends to be pretty territorial." He gestured towards the dog.

Dan thought this over. "You know he is supposed to be under your immediate control, right?" he asked. "Either on a leash or direct voice command." Dan quoted the regulations. "Don't you keep him tied up?"

The man stared at Dan. "Yeah. That's what we do. But you know, sometimes he gets away from us, especially in the evening or night. And I wouldn't want to meet him then, not if I didn't know him really well."

Duke growled on cue. It was not a pretty sound.

"I'll keep that in mind," Dan said. "And you try to make sure that he stays out of trouble, right?"

The man gave a big smile that had no humor in it at all. "Oh, he'll stay out of trouble. It's other people I worry about."

Dan didn't respond. The two men stared at each other for a while.

Dan gave a few pumps on his water filter, slowly and deliberately.

The man turned to walk away. Then he stopped and turned back to Dan. "I have a legal claim up there, filed and notarized. And you better not fuck with it," he said. "Or if you do, you better bring the fuckin' marines. I ain't kiddin'."

He turned and started walking slowly up the hill. Duke stayed where he was, focused completely on Dan. Just when Dan was beginning to get very nervous, the guy turned about and said: "Come on, Duke. Get up here."

The dog stared at Dan and then slowly turned and trotted up to join his master.

Dan kept pumping water until they were both out of sight up the side canyon.

He looked down at his water bottle. It had been full for some time, and Dan was simply pumping water up out the top and back into the stream. He gave his shoulders a little shake to try to pull himself together and reached over to put the cap on his first water bottle. He noticed his hands were shaking. He gave a twist to try to relax his neck and slipped the filter tube into his second water bottle. He noticed that his left calf was beginning to cramp, and he couldn't decide if he should stand up and stretch it out, or finish pumping. The pain grew stronger, and he stood up.

Standing above the stream, he looked around. The sun was getting low in the west—that golden hour when everything looks as if God is smiling on it. Dan took a deep breath and tried to draw it all in. He let the air out, blowing his cheeks out as he did so.

He had enough water. The second bottle wasn't full, but he had enough for dinner. He packed up the filter, grabbed the water bottles, and worked his way back up to his camp. It was now in shade from the west ridge of the canyon, and it was suddenly cooler, almost cold.

Back at his tent, Dan put down the water and dug around in his pack for his vest. He slipped it on and walked over to the bear can. Before he could get it open, his radio crackled at him.

Dan picked up the radio and relayed the afternoon's experiences to Steve Matson. Steve wasn't pleased. "God dammit, Dan, I really need you to be careful up there. If that guy comes out again, I want you to just walk away."

"Steve," Dan pleaded his case. "I was squatting on the stream filtering water when the guy snuck up behind me. Believe me, I was not looking for trouble."

"Okay, okay." Steve acknowledged. "Look, there is a lot going on down here. The Sheriff's tied up with a homicide. I am going to try to get you some back-up tomorrow. Otherwise, just sit tight and keep anyone else away from there. Right?"

"Yep," Dan said. "The guy was pretty sure of himself. He said that if we were going to try to force him to leave, we should bring the Marines."

"Yeah, well, maybe we'll do that," Steve said. "Anyway, sit tight, stay out of the way, and keep me informed about anything that happens. Got it?'

"Yes, I do," Dan replied. "I will do exactly that."

After he got off the radio, Dan turned back to his bear can. His stomach was growling, and he decided that he deserved to eat well tonight. Not only a freeze-dried dinner and some fruit. Tonight he might just eat a whole damn chocolate bar.

chapter 9

Dan did not sleep well that night. He kept thinking that he heard noises near his camp, and while they were probably just the local wildlife, a coyote or deer, Dan couldn't help worry that the miner's dog was back, looking for trouble. Twice he actually turned on his headlamp to scan his surroundings, but he didn't see anything at all, not even a pair of eyes reflecting the light back to him. Twice he turned over and struggled to get back to sleep.

But he had drifted off to a deep sleep when the dawn chorus of birds woke him up. At least that sounded normal, he thought. He scrunched around in his sleeping bag and looked out the mesh door of his tent. It was a beautiful morning. Because he was down in the canyon, it would be a while before the sun hit his tent, but the sky was clear and that deep Sierra blue color that always made Dan happy.

He climbed out of his bag and put some water on to boil. Looking across the canyon, he didn't see anything moving, and felt his blood pressure easing down. At least maybe he was going to be able to eat his breakfast in peace. He poured the oatmeal into his bowl, the cocoa into his mug, and sat back to wait for the water to heat. He remembered his little bag of walnuts and added a few of them to the oatmeal, then grabbed a fistful of craisins and jammed them into his mouth. The bright flavor and acidity seemed to wake him up.

The water was boiling, so Dan added it into his bowl and mug, and started stirring.

That's when the radio squawked at him.

Dan stared at it. It was tempting to ignore it, but Dan knew that Steve Matson would only get angry if he did that. He picked up the radio and answered.

First things first. Steve wanted to know what had happened last night.

"Not much," Dan assured him. "I tried to sleep, and sometimes I was successful."

Steve asked about the miner and his dog.

"Nope, not a peep from them," Dan replied. "Maybe he's just up there, waiting for the Marines."

Steve was silent, and Dan wondered if the radio had gone dead. No such luck.

"So that actually gave me an idea," he heard Matson say. "The Sheriff's Department is so tied up with this homicide, and the PCT traffic issues, that they aren't offering much help."

Dan took this in and resisted the temptation to ask Steve what his solution was. Dan knew that was coming next. And he wasn't looking forward to it.

"But your guy actually gave me the idea," he heard Matson say. "Last night I put in a call to Colonel Perez over at the MWTC." Matson paused to allow Dan to comment.

The Mountain Warfare Training Center was a Marine base on the east side of Sonora Pass. They trained young kids on what it was like to live and fight at high elevation. Dan didn't like where this was going, but he held his tongue.

He heard Matson continue, "Colonel Perez was willing to help us out."

Dan stared at the radio. "What the fuck are you thinking?" he thought to himself. He kept his thumb off the transmitter button of the radio. He would let Matson imagine what he was thinking.

"So your back-up will be a couple of teams of Marines," Matson said. "They're hiking in today and should be there this afternoon."

Dan couldn't hold his tongue any longer. "And what am I supposed to do with a bunch of Marines?" Dan asked. "Should we use a full-frontal assault, with air support, or would you prefer that we simply use mortars and flamethrowers to drive out the insurgents?"

Steve Matson was not amused. "Take it easy, Dan. There are clear rules of engagement that we've agreed on. Colonel Perez insists on that. And the mission is to take those guys at the mine without anyone getting hurt. The colonel thinks this is a good training exercise, because they may have similar missions in the future, in combat."

Dan stared at the radio again. "So these guys are going to come up here, take over from me, take the miners down the mountain, and nobody gets hurt? That doesn't sound very likely to me."

"You in are charge," Matson replied. "The Marines are in a support function. They will not fire unless fired upon, and they will follow your lead, unless they deem it to be unsafe."

Dan snorted. "You mean, I can suggest what they do, and then they'll tell me if they want to do that or not? What if I tell them that the strategy is for them to head back down the mountain and forget this ever happened?"

Steve Matson wasn't pleased with Dan's response. "Dan, you have two choices here. You can stay there and work with the Marines to resolve this situation, or you can leave it in their hands. As soon as you see the first Marines arrive, you can tell them what it is you are going to do."

Dan thought this over. The implied threat, in the back of this, was that Dan would be ceding control and authority over to the Marines. Matson knew Dan well enough to know that Dan would resist that at all costs.

Dan pushed the transmitter button. "So, when they get here, what exactly is the plan? And what kind of authority and responsibility do I have?"

"You're in charge," Matson replied. "You have the right to direct the overall operation. The only caveat is that the Marines can refuse to do anything that they consider unsafe or in violation of the mission, which is to arrest those guys without a loss of life. But you can countermand any order from their CO if you feel it will violate our mission of protecting the wilderness."

Dan thought this over. "This sounds like a colossal circus," he said. "They can refuse to do anything that I say, and I can refuse to allow them to do anything they want. Seems like all we are doing is marching a bunch of boy soldiers up into the mountains so they can dig a few latrines and pitch a few tents."

"That may be all it takes, Dan," Steve Matson responded. "The idea here is to give those guys a real show of force, and that's when I'm hoping we can talk some sense into them."

"No, no, no," Dan heard himself say. "So, you march all these Marines up here, and then it's my fault if something goes wrong? I don't think so."

"I understand how you feel, Dan. I will be heading up there as soon as I can. That may be as early as tomorrow. Until then, all I am asking you to do is to work with the Marines to set up a perimeter around the miners, and make sure that nobody gets hurt."

Dan had a very ugly feeling about this. He kept his finger off the radio button.

Steve Matson waited a few minutes, and then broke the silence. "The officer in charge of the Marine teams is a Captain Lewis. He'll be bringing about ten Marines up the main trail to meet you. Another squad will be hiking up the backside, up Kennedy Canyon, and they'll take positions up on the ridge above the miners on that side. Are we clear exactly where these guys are?"

Dan sighed. He clicked on the radio and gave Steve the GPS coordinates for the side canyon. "You realize that the ridge on the east side there is damn near vertical, right?" he said to Matson.

"Roger that. These guys are trained in mountain warfare. The Colonel has studied this area with his team, and they are confident they can take positions up there, and rappel down if they have to. These guys are pros, Dan."

"No, they're not," Dan responded. "I've met these kids on the trail. They are kids. They carry 80-pound packs and they dig ditches and hike back down again. And they'll have plenty of guns and ammo, I am sure." Dan paused. "This is a horror show waiting to happen, Steve."

"I'll be there tomorrow," Steve answered. "Until then, just sit tight and let these guys set up their perimeter. Talk to Captain Lewis. He is not a kid, and he understands perfectly well what they're getting into. He'll work with you on everything from where to camp to how to set up."

Dan thought it over. Twenty-four hours. If he could make this work for twenty-four hours, then Steve would take over and Dan could get the hell out of here. It seemed doable to him, but he didn't want to make it easy for Steve.

"And what happens if these guys start shooting at us, and the

Marines return fire, and we suddenly have casualties on both sides? Then what?" He waited for Steve to answer.

"The Marines are very clear in the objectives for today," Steve replied. "They'll set up a perimeter to both keep everyone else out, and to make sure these guys don't make a run for it. That's all for today. Tomorrow I should be able to get up there and take over the operation."

Dan still wasn't happy, but he was beginning to admit this might work. "So their only job is to surround the area, right? They will stay out of sight down here with me. No attacks, no gunfights, no shooting at all?"

"That's the plan, Dan," Matson reassured him. "Tomorrow I'll be up there, and we think we can resolve this once we make it clear how badly outnumbered they are."

Dan gave a dry laugh. "Yep. That's a plan all right."

"The Marines should reach you sometime after lunch," Steve answered. "Talk to Captain Lewis, give him the lay of the land, and let him get his men set up. I'll be up there tomorrow."

And in the meantime, Dan thought, I'll be sitting on a can of gunpowder, waiting for it to explode.

He put the radio down and looked at his breakfast. The sun was well up over the ridge now, and his breakfast was stone cold. Dan resisted the impulse to kick the bowl down the mountainside, and sat down on a rock. It was just as cold as his breakfast.

<h1 style="text-align:center">chapter 10</h1>

Dan had never been good at just sitting around. Once he had finished his breakfast, he decided to tidy up his camp. That took about four minutes.

He looked across the canyon where the man he had decided to call Cameron Scott had appeared. He sat on a nearby rock and watched for another ten minutes. Nothing happened. Dan traced a route that he could take up the ridge on the other side of the canyon, where he could possibly see down into the miners' camp. He was sure that it wouldn't take him more than about forty-five minutes to get to the top of the ridge, even taking into account the usual difficulty in estimating distances where there was little to give him a sense of scale.

And when he got to the top of the ridge? What then? He could sit down and watch for a while, but he really couldn't do anything else. Not without deliberately disobeying his boss.

Dan decided that it was way too early in the morning for that.

He turned around and looked at the mountain that rose up behind him. It was just as steep and would probably take him just as long to climb it. But at least he could explain that he was climbing it to check on the hikers he'd seen the day before. He might be able to see them hike down the trail if he hurried. And from up there, he would also have a pretty good view of the Marines as they made their frontal assault on his position.

The thought made him angry enough that he stood up and started hiking up the slope. There was no hiking trail here, of course, just a series of game trails that led one way and then the other. Dan enjoyed the mental exercise of guessing which of them would lead him more directly to the peak, all the while keeping his eyes open for an alternative that might allow him to go straight up without slipping on the exposed scree. Occasionally a rock outcropping broke through the scree, and Dan began to aim for these, knowing that they offered more stable footing.

It felt good to be hiking, to be working this hard. His breath began to get a little ragged as he forced himself up the steep slope, sometimes taking an extra-long step to avoid slipping, other times working over or around the rocks, always aiming for a diagonal path up the steep slope.

He glanced off to his right, down the canyon, and realized that he could now see down into Lunch Meadow, and the meandering stream through it. It looked remarkably peaceful in the morning light. Dan could just barely make out where the trail ran through it, soon to be trampled by Marines.

He turned back to the mountain and started climbing again, this time veering slightly to the right so that he could follow the ridge up to the top. How high was it? He checked his watch and got a reading of 9800 feet. And he still had a short way to go. Would it be over ten K? He would have to check the map when he got back to his camp. He knew his watch wasn't all that accurate.

Near the top the peak leveled out onto a broader ridge, and Dan kept his eyes on the valley to his right. Somewhere down there should be the trail, and he should see that group of hikers soon. He hoped to hell they hadn't decided to come back over Brown Bear

Pass. That would mean he would have to hustle down the slope he'd just climbed to catch them—not something he would enjoy.

And there they were. Dan could see them now, or at least four or five of them. He stopped to count. Five, and all hiking more or less together. And then at the back the sixth hiker came into view. Probably the photographer of the group, Dan figured. They were on the right trail, and he could cross that worry off his list.

From where they were hiking, Dan could now follow the trail almost down into Lunch Meadow. He was grateful to see that there were no Marines yet.

He took a stroll over the top of the peak, taking in the views. Mosquito Lake was right below him, with another peak straight across, and he could see just a small slice of Emigrant Meadow Lake off in the distance. This would be a pretty nice place for lunch, he thought. He wished he'd thought of it sooner, and had packed a lunch when he had left camp. All he had was a water bottle and an energy bar, which he pulled out and immediately consumed.

Looking back over his camp, Dan could see across to Molo and Relief Peaks, towering over the canyon on the north side. Steve Matson had said something about Marines approaching from that side, as well. He wished them good luck. He'd climbed up that canyon once a few years ago and knew how steep it was. There would be snow in the chutes on the north side all summer long, even in a dry year like this one.

Dan checked his watch. If he walked down slowly, he could arrive at his camp more or less around lunchtime. It would be a little early, but in the mountains he was never afraid of eating too soon. All too often, things came up later and then…

Dan headed down the ridge. As he looked down into Lunch Meadow, he couldn't believe his eyes. There was a group of hikers on their way up the trail. Dan watched them for a minute. They were moving awfully fast, compared to the kids he had just seen a few minutes ago. And they were all wearing the same dull, dark earthtone colors.

Marines, it had to be them. Dan watched for a minute or two, amazed that they would keep up the steady pace. Were they jogging up the trail? Dan gave a start and hurried down the mountain. It would not be good form to have them arrive, only to find that he had deserted his post…

In the end, he trotted into camp a few minutes before they arrived. And by the time they arrived, they were no longer jogging, just hiking at a normal pace. He could see their massive packs and noted that they were carrying their rifles in their hands. Dan strode down toward the creek and trail to meet them. He wondered what the group of kids had thought when they ran into these guys up here. Given the situation, he was glad he was in uniform, such as it was.

As he got close to the first Marines, Dan noted that one of them was talking into a radio on his shoulder strap. That soldier looked up at Dan and greeted him, "Ranger Courtwright?"

Dan chuckled quietly to himself and agreed that he was Ranger Courtwright.

"Captain Lewis will be here shortly, sir." The Marine looked as if he were still in high school.

Dan nodded and pointed to his campsite. "You guys might want to set up somewhere nearby," he said. And as he said it, he hoped that they wouldn't set up their camp too close to his own.

After the first few Marines walked by him and threw their packs to the ground, Captain Lewis appeared, complete with his own pack and GI boots. Dan didn't envy their heavy gear.

Captain Lewis looked at least five years older than his troops, and he wasn't carrying a rifle. He extended his hand to Dan and greeted him. "Good to see you, sir."

"Thanks," Dan said. "You guys really hustled up here."

"Yessir, we were told to make all due speed."

Dan was impressed and he said so.

Lewis threw down his pack, slightly apart from those of his men, Dan noted, and turned back around. Dan could see his eyes scanning the canyon behind him. The Marine pointed to the stream coming down the side of the canyon and said: "That's where these guys are holed up?"

Dan agreed.

Lewis' eyes kept roving over the side of the canyon. "That's a narrow entry point." He paused and scanned the rest of the canyon-side. "Have you been up there to see what it looks like on the other side?" he asked.

Dan explained that he had been expressly directed not to do that.

Lewis nodded. "And you said that you thought you saw some kind of installation or electronics over there?"

Dan explained how he had seen what he thought were solar panels, and pointed out Brown Bear Pass, where he had been standing.

Captain Lewis spoke into his shoulder strap and asked for an update on position from someone. Dan couldn't hear the response and realized that the other man had some kind of earpiece in one ear. "Roger that," Captain Lewis turned back to Dan.

"As I see this situation," he explained to Dan, "these guys have more intel on us than we have on them. And I don't like that equation." He turned around and called to a few of his men. Dan began to realize that there were least ten, maybe twelve Marines in his camp now. Steve Matson had said there would be ten.

As some of the young men gathered around their commander, Lewis spoke to Dan, "We're going to change that equation as soon as we can. I've got another squad that's climbing up the ridge behind these miners, and they should be in position in about ninety minutes, by their estimate. Meanwhile, I am going to take out that installation that you noticed. That will reduce their ability and intel, while increasing our own."

Dan thought about this. "Could you explain exactly what you mean when you say that you are going to take out that installation?" he asked. He had a vision of large explosions and didn't like it at all.

Captain Lewis nodded, and responded with a very measured tone. "We are going to send a couple of men up there to pick it up and carry it out of there, if you agree." Dan thought he saw just the smallest hint of a smile flicker across Lewis' face.

"Yeah, that sounds good," Dan heard himself saying, and feeling a little foolish.

Captain Lewis then started issuing orders faster than Dan could keep up. Some of the Marines were directed to set up camp. They were told to check with Dan as to where and how to do that. Two others were directed to listen to Dan as he explained exactly where the solar panels were located. While Dan was busy explaining to more Marines than he had ever personally met in his life, he heard Captain Lewis directing three of his men to climb the ridge across the canyon and report back what they could see. And another two were sent to position themselves high above the supposed solar panels, to provide cover for the two men who were going to remove it.

That startled Dan back to reality. He asked Captain Lewis to explain how that was going to work.

Lewis looked straight at Dan. "I need to make sure that I am not sending my men into a dangerous situation," he said. "The first team will take up positions above those panels, higher on the slopes, where they can see anyone who is coming down that creek from their side. Once they are in position, the men removing the equipment will be protected."

Dan had to admit this made sense, but he was still concerned. "And if those guys in the first team run into problems?" he asked.

"Our orders, as directed by Supervisor Matson, are to avoid any direct conflict, and return fire only if and when we are directly threatened and fired upon. Our mission is to remove the miners with no loss of life on either side."

Dan nodded, and then looked around at the young Marines, all carrying a massive amount of weaponry, and looking at Dan expectantly.

"Okay," he said. "Let's just make sure that everybody understands that."

"Yessir," Lewis agreed. "We are clear on that." The Marines around him nodded at Dan.

"Okay," Dan said. "Let's go take out that crap."

Lewis looked at him carefully. Dan stared back, then raised his hand up softly and added, "and I will observe from here."

Lewis nodded, and the men burst into action.

chapter 11

It didn't take long. Within half an hour, Captain Lewis was getting reports from his men up on the ridge across the canyon. They couldn't see exactly where the miners were, but they could eliminate large areas of the canyon. The men who took up positions above the solar panels could not see any sign of miners or mining from where they were, but they could see far enough up the canyon to protect the team below.

Ten minutes later, the solar panels and a couple of bags full of electronics were being hoisted up by the Marines. As Dan watched them hike back down towards the creek, he heard Captain Lewis on the radio. Dan turned to look at him.

"The team on the far ridge are roping up for safety," Lewis explained. "They estimate another hour or so to get into position. But one team has found a route that should get them there sooner."

Dan nodded. "I thought they might want to do that," he said. "That's pretty tough climbing over there, especially with the kind of gear you guys carry."

"We're trained for it," Lewis replied. "Once they get into position, we'll have a much better idea of what our next steps can be."

The two Marines with the bags of equipment had now crossed the stream, and were climbing up towards Dan.

One of them called out, "Couple of solar panels, a storage battery, a couple of electric eyes set up on the rocks up there… maybe a camera. There was a camera, but I don't think it was linked to anything. The electric eye was hooked up to a transmitter, but it only had one channel open."

Dan looked at Captain Lewis.

"He's actually a pretty good computer guy," Lewis said. "But he wanted to do something more with his life." He pulled out a canteen and drank. Then he turned and told the last few men in camp to make sure they were drinking as well.

"Yessir!" was the chorused reply.

Dan directed his gaze off into the distance and tried to look thoughtful. There was no question that he had never been attracted to serving in the military, and the idea of such a rigid command structure made his skin crawl. He had grave misgivings about this whole operation. But he also had to admit that so far, the Marines had absolutely lived up to their billing. They were organized and efficient. Dan just hoped things stayed this calm.

Forty-five minutes later, Captain Lewis had his team in position up on the ridge between Molo and Relief Peaks. In addition to spotting scopes and binoculars, they had also carried up an audio listening device.

Dan was skeptical. "They must be something like a mile away," he said. "Can they actually hear anything from that far away?"

Captain Lewis smiled. "It all depends on the acoustics," he said.

"So right now, my men can see two individuals in the canyon," Lewis explained. "There are two tents set up right about here." He pointed to a spot on his map.

"And it looks like there are some mining works over here." He pointed to an area closer to the creek. "We can't be sure that there are only two individuals. My men can see at least two rifles; both look like hunting rifles rather than military arms. But there could be more in the tents. More men, or more arms."

Dan asked if they could see the dog, and Lewis relayed this message over the radio. He listened for a moment, then turned to Dan.

"They think they can see the dog lying down near one of the tents," he said. "At this point, there is no indication that they are aware of our activity at all. The individuals seem to be talking, not mining."

Now what? Dan thought. We've got them surrounded, but they don't know it. And we're a long way from a solution.

Dan jumped when his radio squawked at him. He glanced at Captain Lewis and hoped he hadn't noticed.

Steve Matson wanted an update. Dan gave it to him and was relieved to hear that Steve was in Kennedy Meadows and was hiring a mule to take him up the trail this afternoon. He expected to arrive before dark. Unlike the Marines' radios, this one was loud enough that everyone could hear what Dan was hearing.

"With any luck, that's my ticket out of here," Dan said. "With Steve here, you won't need me."

Lewis nodded, somewhat vacantly, to Dan. Dan realized that the Marine was getting an update from his observer crew through his earbuds.

"Okay," Lewis said. "One of the individuals has left camp, heading due west along the contours. If he doesn't change course, he is going to run into a couple of our men in about twenty or thirty minutes."

Dan asked if the man was armed.

"I can't confirm that," Captain Lewis said, "but he is not carrying a rifle. He might have a sidearm." He talked quietly into his radio, then waited for a response. Then spoke again. The only thing Dan could hear for sure was the final "Roger that."

Dan looked expectantly at him. "With some luck, our friend is going to walk right past our positions up there and continue to hike down towards the trailhead. And if he does, we'll wait until he passes our men, and then stop him."

Dan thought this over. "And if he suddenly starts firing at your men?"

"They will defend themselves," Lewis replied. "But having four Marines suddenly announce their presence from your rear doesn't usually result in immediate gunfire. My guess is that the sonofabitch is going to be so surprised he'll just drop down on the ground and play dead."

"Let's hope so," Dan said, with a healthy dose of skepticism.

Captain Lewis' eyes once again indicated that he was getting information from the radio. After the usual back and forth into the microphone, he turned back to Dan.

"The other individual went into the tent and came out quickly with a rifle. He called the dog, and they are now walking out towards us along the creek."

Dan looked across at where the Marines had been stationed to protect the removal operation. He thought he could see one of them, but not the rest.

"Are those guys still up there?" he asked.

Lewis nodded. "We may get both of these guys to walk right into our arms."

Dan looked confused.

"You told them that the trail was closed, right?" Lewis asked him. Dan nodded. "My guess is that the one guy is going to try to get back down to the trailhead and get supplies. He's taken that route to avoid letting you know what he's doing."

Dan considered this.

"The other individual may have noticed that his transmitter was not working," Lewis continued. "So, one guy to get resupplies, and the other to check on the alarm system."

Lewis turned to the men in camp and ordered some of them to take all of the confiscated equipment and place it in clear view down by the stream. The rest he ordered to take all of their packs and get them out of sight as well as possible.

He turned to Dan. "I want him to think that you took that stuff away. Because I want him to come right up here to talk to you about it." As he was talking, he began to slowly move away from Dan, finally sitting down where Dan had hidden his backpack yesterday.

Dan looked at him. "So, I'm the bait?'

Lewis smiled. "Yeah, but he won't make it to this side of the creek before my men take him under control. Your job is to stand there and look determined."

Dan face broke into a laugh. "I'll see what I can do." Then he thought about the dog. "And what about the dog?"

"Let's just hope he keeps barking," Lewis replied. "I don't want to have to shoot him. But our orders are about the men, not about the dog."

Dan turned and looked across the canyon. Now he could see two of the Marines. One, higher up on the hillside, was motioning to one of the men lower down.

Dan could hear birds calling, and the creek quietly gurgling below. They waited.

Dan realized he was holding his breath. He heard Captain

Lewis call over to him quietly, "First individual has been captured without incident. He is in custody and sitting tight right now."

Dan held his thumb up towards the officer, then looked back across the canyon. The sun was now beginning to drop, and Dan could see that the shadows were ever so slightly beginning to lengthen on his side of the canyon. The other side was still in full sun.

And then he saw Cameron Scott, walking slowly down to where his solar panels had been installed. Scott stared at the ground, bending over to pick up something, then stood up and looked across at Dan, shielding his eyes from the sun as he did so. Dan didn't know if he should wave or what, so he just stared back.

Up on the hillside, he could see one Marine watching Scott, aiming this rifle at him from above.

Cameron Scott began to walk down the small creek, heading straight for the bottom of the canyon, and straight towards Dan. He looked angry and he was walking with a purpose.

Captain Lewis stood up and walked out from behind the rock. At his signal, the rest of the Marines in camp came out from their hiding places and stood with Dan.

Cameron Scott halted and stared. He called to his dog and put a leash on the huge animal. Dan thought this was a good sign. Scott stood still, staring at the sight of the men across the canyon. He clearly didn't know what to do. They let him walk down another fifty yards.

Dan heard Captain Lewis speak into his mic. The four marines on the hillside behind Scott stood up and announced their presence to Cameron Scott.

Scott slowly placed his rifle on the ground and then held his hands over his head. Two of the Marines hurried down the hillside to direct him towards camp. They stayed on opposite sides of Scott, slowly walking him down to the bottom of the canyon. The dog, Dan noted, was barking frantically, but didn't know which way to turn.

"You'll need to tie that dog up to this tree over here," Dan heard Lewis say. "We would appreciate that. We do not want to be forced to hurt him."

Scott tied his dog to a nearby tree, where it growled and barked at anyone and everyone.

When a third Marine came down the slope with Scott's rifle, Dan turned to Captain Lewis.

Lewis smiled at him. "Did you say that Supervisor Matson was going to arrive this evening?" he asked with a smile.

Dan nodded, then chuckled. "Yes, he is."

"Good," said Lewis. "We'll be able to make a full report then."

Dan laughed. "I could call him on the radio right now," he said.

Lewis shook his head. "It's your call, sir. But in my opinion that would ruin the surprise."

Dan turned to watch some of the Marines already turn their attention to collecting their gear.

"Are you guys going to hike out of here tonight?" he asked.

Captain Lewis shook his head. "We could do that, but I'm not sure our prisoner is up to that. We'll camp here and head out in the morning, unless we get other orders."

Dan nodded. That was exactly what he would do, too.

chapter 12

By the time that Steve Matson arrived, Dan's plans had changed.

"Somehow these guys got word out to a whole bunch of nut cases," Matson told him. "They're coming in from all over the country, and I want to get him out of here as soon as possible. I want him back down in Sonora or Stockton by tonight."

Dan and Captain Lewis exchanged looks and nodded. "We're ready to roll when you are," Lewis assured him.

Steve looked at Dan. "I'd like you to stay up here to keep an eye on things, Dan," he said. "Take stock of what kind of a mess they've created up here and document that. We'll close off the trailhead back at Kennedy Meadows, so that should keep everyone else away."

Dan didn't really mind staying in the backcountry another day or two, but he did have a dinner date with Kristen that he was going to miss. He didn't like that, and he was afraid she wouldn't like it at all. With their schedules, finding time together was always a challenge.

Matson looked at the Marine officer. "I think you've got a couple of people who are good with canines?"

"Yes, sir, I do," Lewis agreed.

"If you could ask them to try to manage that dog and get him down the mountain, that would be a big help."

Lewis agreed again. "Yes, sir, we'll do that."

Within fifteen minutes Dan and two Marines were left alone as the rest of the group, including Matson on a mule, were packed up and hiking back down the trail. Dan looked at the two young men. One was a thin black man with glasses and a ready smile. His uniform said he was Jackson. The other, Hispanic or possibly Native American, had Begay on his name tag.

Dan turned to the two Marines and held out his hand. "I'm Dan."

"Yes, sir!" the Marines responded. "Begay, sir," one replied. The other shook Dan's hand and said, "Jackson, sir!"

Dan considered trying to convince these two young men to call him something other than "sir" and decided it probably wasn't worth the effort. "You guys are good with dogs?" He knew the answer before it was given

"Yes, sir!" they chorused.

Dan looked at the first Marine. "Begay? Are you Navajo?"

"I'm a Marine, sir!" the soldier replied. Then, with an apologetic smile, "And yeah, Navajo. From Tuba City."

Dan chuckled. "Great. So, if you guys will manage that wild dog of his, I'll give you a few minutes, then see if I can get to work."

Begay looked at Dan carefully. "It may take us more than a few minutes to manage his dog, sir. We're good, but this might take some time."

Dan sighed. "Okay. I'll wait here, and you tell me when you think it's clear for me to come up there."

"Yes, sir!" The Marines turned and marched up the slope toward the miner's dog.

Dan sat down on a rock near his tent and waited. He pulled out his radio and checked in with Carmen in dispatch. He had to be careful, because he knew that Steve Matson could hear the conversation. But he asked Carmen to let Doris know he wouldn't be in for another couple of days. And he hoped that Doris would put two and two together and give Kristen a call.

By the time he was done, he heard a whistle, and looked over to see Jackson waving to him.

Dan hopped up and climbed up past the waterfall to see the miner's camp. Jackson explained that the dog was now chained up and that private Begay was giving him water and food. Dan should be able to walk around to the far side of the camp and look over the mining operation.

As Dan climbed up higher into the side canyon, the full operation came into view. There were a couple of yellow tents set up on a bench above the stream, and the dog, and Begay, were nearby, seeming to get along for now. Dan hoped his own presence wouldn't mess that up.

But up above the camp the canyon was a mess. The miners had dug up a long swath of the grass alongside the creek to get at the gravel below, and it had left a huge scar in the little canyon. On the near side of the creek Dan could see the mine tailings, left over gravel and rocks that had been washed and then dumped in huge piles on top of the grass to get them out of the way.

His stomach gave a lurch to see how much of the little canyon had been damaged. It would take years and years for it to recover, and that could only happen after they got a CEQA plan approved for the work. Dan figured that the earliest that could happen might be next summer.

His sigh attracted the attention of Jackson, who had come over to stand near him. "You want us to start trying to move all the dirt back again?" Jackson asked.

Dan shook his head. "Nah. We can't touch it. First we have to figure out where it should all go, and how it fits together. We need a plan to make sure we don't affect the stream hydraulics…" His voice faded out as he thought about it all. "This is going to be a long, slow process…the fuckers."

The look on Jackson's face showed Dan that he was disappointed and clearly wanted to help.

At the far end of the cut, Dan could see a whole strip of vegetation that had been cut up and stacked above the stream, exposing the gravel. But the miners hadn't started mining that part.

Dan looked at the young Marine. "Let's not tell anyone that we're doing this," he said.

The Marine smiled and replied, "Yes, sir!"

After taking a few photos for documentation, Dan and the young Marine went to work. However hard Dan tried, he realized that he could not keep up with the younger man, and by the end of the afternoon, they had replaced most of the sod that had been recently stripped off the soil. It wasn't a perfect job, but Dan figured that with a little rain and some luck, the vegetation would root itself pretty quickly and recover. At least that was better than leaving it all winter this way. There were still the tailings and the lower part of the cut that were exposed.

He turned to Jackson and held out his hand. "Thank you" he said.

"Yes, sir!" came the inevitable reply.

As they walked back down towards the miners' camp, they could see that Begay was sitting next to the dog, holding it on a short leash.

"You guys go on ahead," Begay called to them, as he struggled to hold the dog. "I may join you later, or just hike down on my own. He's fine, but I don't think he likes the ranger, sir."

Dan nodded. "Wouldn't be the first time," he responded. And he headed back to camp.

By the time he got there, his radio squawked again. Plans had changed. Dan should hike out the next morning. There was a lot going on, and Dan was needed to help out. In fact, could he hike out tonight?

Dan looked at Jackson, who was pretending not to listen, then glanced at his watch. "I don't like hiking this trail in the dark," he responded. "But I can probably get to the reservoir and hike out early tomorrow morning."

And with a sigh, he signed off the radio, and started packing up his gear.

He thanked the two young Marines one more time, and started hiking back down the trail towards Relief Reservoir. He knew at least two different spots where he could camp along the way, and hoped that at least one of them wasn't occupied.

Dan was surprised how light his pack felt as his feet hit the trail. Then he realized it wasn't his pack, but his heart. He took a deep breath of the clean mountain air and increased his stride down the canyon.

When he got to the first campsite, it was still light enough for Dan to consider hiking on. The site was deeply shaded, surrounded by lodgepole pines, and Dan knew that there would be mosquitoes in numbers once the sun went down.

He kept hiking.

The second spot was on a bare ridge with a clear view of the reservoir. Dan knew that it was a long way down to get water here, so he dropped his pack in a conspicuous place near the fire ring and took his filter and water bottles down a steep ravine to the lake. It was a brushy bushwhack, with an occasional slippery granite slope, but he made it down and got back with enough water for dinner, breakfast, and the hike out.

Back at camp, he set up his tent and had the stove going to boil water in minutes. He opened the miso soup packet, and the freeze-dried dinner package, and laid out his bowl and spoon.

And then it was time to wait for the water to boil.

He looked up and allowed his eyes to take in the scene around him. The sun was down now, and the trees were black against the sky. The blue of the lake reflected the impossible blue of the sky. A couple of pink clouds to the West mirrored the pink slabs of granite on the slopes around him. The air wasn't quite still, but even the tops of the trees were motionless, as if the air was so light and clear that it couldn't move them.

A sound broke the reverie, and Dan realized that the water in his pot was boiling. Time for a quick dinner and then into bed.

<h1 style="text-align:center">chapter 13</h1>

The next morning, when he hiked back into Kennedy Meadows, Dan was surprised to see that that it was a lot quieter than he expected. The usual hustle and bustle seemed subdued, and Dan figured that was a good thing. The sun warmed him up as he walked across the dirt of the stable area, causing a small cloud of dust to rise behind him.

It wasn't until he got to his parked truck that he suspected something else may have been going on. Voices from the campground across the way came to him in hushed tones, and he could just make out a few flashing lights out closer to the highway.

Once he arrived there, he realized that Tuolumne County law enforcement and CHP cars had blocked the road, forcing him to stop.

A young sheriff officer smiled and waved him through. Dan rolled down his window and nodded to the officer. "You guys seem to have this under control," he said. "Where are all of our vigilantes who want to take up mining all of a sudden?"

"Nobody gets in unless they have a wilderness permit or a campground reservation," the young officer replied. "So far we haven't had any trouble—but I think most of the group that said they were driving up here have decided to stop in Sonora and have a drink."

Dan waited while another officer moved a traffic cone to let him pass.

A radio crackled, and the first young LEO held out his hand to stop Dan.

"Sorry, I've been asked to hold you up here," he said. "Do you have some kind of ID?"

Dan gave an audible sigh and reached into his back pocket for his wallet.

From behind his car he heard a voice call out, "Did you sleep in those clothes?"

He glanced in the side mirror to see Cal Healey walking up behind his car.

Dan chuckled. "Nope. I brought my Bugs Bunny sleepers up there."

Cal laughed. "Yeah, I figured you would."

"Man, this is quite a rodeo," Dan said.

"You don't know the half of it," Cal replied. "How long have you been out of the office? Did you hear about the guy we found?"

Dan shook his head, glancing over at two other officers who were trying hard to look like they weren't eavesdropping.

"You're gonna get briefed on it pretty soon," Cal continued. "About the time that you decided to go earn your camping merit badge, we got a call about a body down in a canyon back behind Big Hill Road. Pretty ugly scene there."

Dan chose to ignore the crack about camping and waited for him to continue. A car of tourists, fishermen, pulled up and Dan and Cal watched as the two young officers turned them away.

"So, how'd you like camping with the Marines?" he asked. "Did they wake you up for push-ups at oh-dark-thirty?" Cal said.

"They were up and back so fast they never had time to set up camp," Dan said.

"Made you look like a real slacker, huh?" Cal asked him.

Dan took this in without comment. He and Cal watched the fishermen slowly turn around and drive off, clearly muttering to themselves.

"So are you done with your harassment, or should I stick around here and help you defend the forest from some old guys who want to fish the river? They can be pretty dangerous, you know."

"Hey, you're the one who called the Marines," Cal said.

Dan laughed "Not my decision, but they sure made things easy. I guess they're on their way home now?" Dan asked.

"Oh, I don't think so," Cal said. "The shit show is just beginning, and I'll bet they all get to play."

Dan knew the best way to get Cal to talk was to wait him out.

"So we've got the loonies coming up here from Sonora to free Cameron Scott." Cal started counting off on his fingers. "That's the guy you found digging for El Dorado up there." He glanced at Dan.

Dan nodded. "Yeah, I knew that part."

"But what you don't know," Cal continued, "is about the guy we found down off Big Hill Road. They are not giving out any information about him at all. Beat up—I mean really beat up, maybe with a sledgehammer or something—and then they tried to burn the body in the shaft of an old mine out there. So now we've got the FBI here."

One of the officers made a small sound behind Dan, clearly reacting to Cal's information.

"A sledgehammer?" Dan asked. "How many times do you have to hit a guy with a sledgehammer to kill him? What was that all about?"

Cal gave a grunt. "The coroner says that it looks like they tied him up, and then mashed on his feet with the sledgehammer, and not just once but a few times. Then they whacked him on the head with it, and tossed him down into the mine, poured some gas on him, and set him on fire."

"Jesus," Dan muttered. "So if they burned the body, how did they ID him—dental records or something?"

Cal shook his head. "Unless you have an idea of who it could be, dental records aren't much help. And no, no ID on him," Cal said. "And he was pretty badly burned."

Dan thought this over. "Suspects?" he asked.

"Oh hell, they've got a million ideas," Cal explained. "That's why the Feds are here. I don't know. I do know that crime scenes around here don't usually look like that. It was clean. Nothing at all. Not even tire tracks—they had been brushed out. The whole thing."

"How did they even know he was there?" Dan asked. "I mean, if the body was down in a mine…"

"Yeah, well, you can thank your local neighborhood watch," Cal replied.

Dan was stunned, "On Big Hill Road?" he asked incredulously.

"Nice older couple out for a walk," Cal said. "They have a little cabin up there, and they don't know much about the rest of their neighbors. Anyway, they walk down an old logging road, looking for this old mine. Apparently, that's a hobby the guy has, finding old mines. So, as he's parking on Big Hill, he sees a big black SUV come driving down the road. Tinted windows, the whole deal."

"Could be a drug dealer," Dan suggested.

Cal pointed over to the black SUVs parked nearby. "Or an FBI agent. Or a congressman."

Dan chuckled.

"As I was saying… So then they hike down to the mine, and

they smell something burning. So they called that in to Cal Fire right away," Cal continued. "CDF found the guy by following the smell."

"Nice," Dan said with a grimace. "And there's a connection with the SUV?"

"That's one of about a thousand things that we don't know," Cal answered. He looked over at the black SUVs. "But with any luck, these guys are going to fix that."

Dan thought this over. "So how long are you here?"

Cal checked his watch. "I've got a few more hours, then I head up to Sonora Pass to ride herd on the PCT traffic... only I am supposed to keep my eyes open for what they call 'anything suspicious.'"

"If something doesn't smell right to you, it's probably a PCT hiker," Dan said with a smile.

"Ha," Cal replied mirthlessly. "Ha, and ha."

Dan said that he thought he'd head home and get a shower, if that was okay with the Sheriff's Department.

"Hell, yes," Cal said. "Highly recommended by all county authorities, including the health department. And if you want to join me for dinner up at Sonora Pass, Maggie packed enough food for a small army."

Dan thought about the food in his fridge. Then he remembered his date with Kristen. "Thanks, but I think I have a better offer."

Cal looked at him carefully. "Something I should tell Maggie about?"

Dan smiled and rolled up his window, then slowly drove past the collection of officers and vehicles that lined both sides of the road.

<h1 style="text-align:center">chapter 14</h1>

He stopped in at the Summit Ranger Station, where Doris greeted him with a big smile.

"I am so glad that's over!" she said to Dan.

"Yeah, well, it may just be beginning," Dan replied. "Turns out that some of Cameron Scott's friends think they should organize some kind of protest or rescue or something…"

"Oh, no…" Doris' face fell. "I was hoping we could get back to normal now."

Dan laughed out loud. "Doris, you tell me what normal is, and I'll tell you when we get there again."

He began to thumb through the messages on his desk. Doris passed him one more and said, "Kristen just called about twenty minutes ago. She was trying to find you."

The note was short. She had a job to start immediately and would have to take a rain check on dinner. Dan picked up the phone and called her number.

Kristen answered on the first ring, "Hi, Dan. I am so sorry, but I really have to take this job. It's enough money to get me through the rest of the summer, and it's only for about a week."

Dan said that he understood. He didn't really. He wished she had turned it down, but he also knew he was being selfish about it. "So what are you going to be doing?'

"It's a research team from the University of Nevada Reno that's going into the East Fork of the Carson, studying the trout there."

Dan was tempted to offer to accompany her. It was a beautiful area that didn't get a lot of traffic. But instead he wished her a good trip, and hoped that they could have dinner when she got back. He let the question dangle. Should he say more?

There was an awkward silence. Kristen broke it by saying that she would hold him to that promise. It sounded sincere to Dan. He hoped it was.

With Doris in the background, Dan didn't want to say much more. They wished each other well, and Dan hung up the phone. He stared at the messages. One was from Steve Matson. It said that he should take the rest of the day off.

Dan thought that sounded like a good idea.

Doris asked him if everything was okay. "Yep," Dan replied. "But I am going to take Steve's advice and take the rest of the day off. If you need me, it'll have to wait until tomorrow."

"Good," Doris agreed. "I've got Stacy on her way here to help, and we'll be fine."

Dan climbed into his truck and headed back down the mountain. In half an hour he was walking into his house. Four minutes later he was stepping into a hot shower. The hot water helped, but it didn't wash away his disappointment about the rest of the evening. It was going to be a lot less interesting than he had hoped.

Later in the afternoon, after a short nap and a quick check on the news, Dan saw his elderly neighbor Ruth working her way up the driveway with a few newspapers under her arm. Dan got up and opened the door before she had a chance to knock.

"Hi, Dan," she said, looking up at him through thick lenses. "I thought you might like to catch up on the news." She handed him a stack of papers.

Dan thanked her and invited her in.

"Oh, no," she said. "I know you're busy. And Walt is waiting for his dinner."

Walt was her husband of some fifty-five years.

Dan smiled. "Thanks for my evening's entertainment," he said.

"Well, it's not much," Ruth said. "But at least you can catch up on all the sports. I guess you've been gone for a day or two."

Dan nodded. "Yep. Up by Kennedy Meadows."

"Do you have anything to eat for dinner tonight?" Ruth asked.

Dan assured her that he was all set. Plenty of food, and lots of it ready to eat.

Ruth caught him staring at the top newspaper in the stack. "Terrible story," she said. "They found someone murdered out by Big Hill Road. Just awful."

Dan looked at the paper. That was one story he might read with more interest.

"Is that in the national forest?" Ruth asked. "Is that something you have to bother with?"

"I think that one is with the Sheriff's Department," Dan said. "At least, that's what I've been told."

"Oh, good," said Ruth. "Terrible story."

Dan thanked her again and asked her to give his best to Walt.

"I will, honey," Ruth said. "But I'll probably have to wait for a break in the ballgame."

Dan laughed and thanked her one more time.

And then, after he had closed the door, he opened up the newspaper and began to read. He didn't learn much he didn't already know, but the writer had done a good job of making the whole thing seem as violent and sensational as possible.

Dan sighed. It would probably turn out to be the usual drug deal gone bad. He looked at the clock and decided that it was time for an early night.

And then the phone rang.

chapter 15

Dan allowed the call to go to his answering machine, where he heard the caller say, "Dan, it's Bruce. How's it going? I thought you might want an update on our mining project. I've got some good news. Give me a call and I'll bring you up to speed."

Dan stared at the machine.

His ex-brother-in-law was not the person Dan wanted to talk to. Still, he was intrigued by the message. Had Bruce really managed to get some gold out of that old claim? Why else would he have called?

Dan knew at least ten people in Tuolumne County who were trying to mine for gold in one way or another, and that didn't count the old Lost Dutchman gang that worked the river down there as a group, or the more serious commercial operations.

As far as he knew, none of them were really making any money, although he knew full well that any miner who made money would certainly not tell anyone else about it.

Still, in a small community like this, word inevitably got around. And Dan hadn't heard a peep. He wished he had asked Ruth about it. She might not know, but Walt knew just about everybody, and listened more than he talked. That made him an excellent source of local news.

Dan picked up the phone and called Bruce.

"I thought that message might get your attention," Bruce

enthused. "Want to know what's going on?"

Dan still couldn't get past the sense that Bruce was always selling something to him. But he admitted that he wanted to know about the mining project.

"You were right about getting down in there," Bruce said. "That was a bitch. If I didn't have a good reason to get down all the way to the river, I would have just given up."

Dan chuckled. "I think this is where I get to say I told you so."

"Oh yeah, you told me," Bruce admitted. "But I already knew that. I mean, that's what made this whole thing attractive to me. If it's hard to get to, it's hard to mine. And that means that there might still be some gold there. Keeps out the riff-raff."

Dan smiled. "You may be underestimating those old-time miners, Bruce," he said. "They didn't let much get in their way." He wasn't sure Bruce didn't fit the description of riff-raff anyway.

"Yeah, but Dan, this was a fucking nightmare," Bruce said. "I figure it took me all day to get down there, and it's only about six miles."

"And I'll bet you had some fun with poison oak, too," Dan suggested.

"Everywhere," Bruce admitted. "I was scrambling and sliding, and at the same time doing a dance around every goddam leaf of it."

"That sounds like it would have been fun to watch," Dan said.

"Yeah, well it wasn't fun to do," Bruce shot back. "But the good news is that I did get down there, with a shovel and a pan."

"I'm impressed," Dan told him. "I thought you might not make it."

"Oh, no, you don't know me, Dan," Bruce said. "I don't give up."

"So did you get any gold?" Dan asked.

"It took me longer to get down there than I thought it would, so

I only had one full day to work. Because I knew it was going to take me another whole day to climb back out of there."

"Did you take a GPS?" Dan asked. "At least you knew where you were going on the way back out."

"Yeah, not that it helped much," Bruce said." Usually, it was just figuring out how I was going to get up the next twenty feet."

"And around the poison oak," Dan said.

"Exactly." Bruce sounded exhausted.

"So did you get any gold?" Dan asked again.

Bruce gave a sigh. "I got some," he said. "Not as much as I had hoped, but I got some color in some of the pans. And I was working with limited time. I didn't really get to work it the way I should."

"Welcome to gold mining," Dan said.

"Yeah, I know that," Bruce said. "But I also saw some areas down there that I want to explore a little more. There's one spot with some deep pools that should have some gold in the bottom."

Dan considered this. "How are you planning to do that?" he asked. "Scuba gear? I don't think that would be much fun to drag down into that canyon."

"Not without a mule team," Bruce admitted. "Or someone to help me."

Dan laughed. "Count me out. And I don't think you'd get anyone to lead a team of mules down there either."

"Yeah, I know," Bruce said. "I'm just thinking out loud. I'm going to take a snorkel and mask down there next time and see if that will help."

Dan chuckled. "That water is damn cold."

"Yeah, I know. I was in it, remember?"

"So," Dan tried one more time. "How much gold did you get?"

"I don't know," Bruce waffled. "Just a little. Like maybe three or four grams."

Dan quickly tried to do the math. "And that in a full day of panning?" he asked.

"Well, yeah, but remember, I didn't really get to the good parts yet."

"Say four grams a day," Dan suggested. "If you go down there for a week, that's one day in, three days mining, and one day out. Three days times four grams give you twelve grams for the week. Roughly half an ounce. What's that, $700?"

"Well, yeah, if I do it that way. . ." Bruce admitted.

"Thirty-five grand a year," Dan summed up. "And that's if you mine fifty weeks a year, winter included."

"Yeah, but I was thinking I might set up my work schedule to work four days a week, and then take some three-day weekends to get down there and mine. Think of it as supplemental income."

"Which means you're only mining one of those days," Dan reminded him. "The other two are getting in and out. So one day a week, and maybe only doing it for half the year? That means twenty-five weeks times four grams—a bit less than four ounces."

"Exactly!" Bruce said. "That's like six to ten grand. And it's tax-free!"

Dan laughed. "It's only tax-free if you don't declare the income, Bruce."

"Exactly!" Bruce agreed again. "Pretty cool, huh?"

"Yeah," Dan agreed dryly. "Pretty cool."

chapter 16

The next morning, Dan was on his way up to Sonora Pass to help monitor the PCT hikers. He drove right by the ranger station without stopping. He didn't want to get sidetracked today. He cruised past, noting whose cars were in the lot, and especially enjoyed the last part of the drive where the road climbs up out of Kennedy Meadows and wanders along tiny Deadman Creek, following it high up towards its source. The sun was out, there were still a few patches of snow high on the peaks, and the meadows were still green and lush.

As he drove by the St. Mary's Pass trailhead, he looked for Kristen's Subaru, but didn't see it. She might not have arrived yet. Or she was going to take another trail in. Or she might be part of a pack train if it was a week-long trip. None of that made him feel any better.

There was enough activity around Sonora Pass that Dan had to slowly creep into the parking area, and only found a spot to park when someone offered to move some of the folding chairs to one side to let him in.

Dan counted six tents in all, and about the same number of cars. Someone had set up a few folding tables, and there were drinks and snacks set out on one of them. Dan guessed that there were something like ten to fifteen people milling around.

He was delighted to see Cal Healey was one of them. He was

holding a large cup of coffee and seemed to be chatting with a couple of the trail angels—possibly the ones who had brought the coffee.

Cal smiled and waved him over to a pair of folding chairs underneath the trees. "There's plenty of coffee, if you're interested," he called out to Dan, pointing out a huge urn on one of the tables. As Dan got closer, Cal said in a lower voice, "It's not great coffee, but it's hotter than hell."

Dan chuckled. He passed up the coffee and settled into a chair next to Cal. "Good to see you working hard," he said to Cal. "But I thought you hated this part…"

"Oh, this beats the shit out of what the other guys are doing today," Cal said.

Dan waited for more explanation, but Cal just took a sip of coffee.

"Okay, I'll bite," he said. "What are the other guys doing?"

"They are up to their assholes in an abandoned mine, digging in dirt and mud," Cal said.

Dan looked at Cal in surprise. "It's not like you to pass up working on a crime scene to patrol a parking lot."

"And they're being supervised by at least three FBI agents." Cal added. "I'll bet they are having the time of their lives."

Dan thought this over. Normally the Sheriff's Office would handle local crime. "Let me guess," he said. "It's a drug deal gone bad, and the FBI has been tracking the guy for months."

Cal snorted. "Probably. But you don't imagine that the FBI would tell us that, do you?" He paused. "Or anything else, for that matter? Nope. Just get in there and dig, boys."

Dan considered this. "Do they have an ID on the body yet?"

Cal shook his head. "Nothing so far." A look of disgust passed over his face. "They have no idea who they are looking for."

"Too soon for DNA, even if he's in the database, right?" Dan asked.

Cal nodded and took another sip of coffee. Dan was considering whether the coffee or Cal was hotter at that exact moment.

"Any hardened criminals passing through on the PCT?" he asked mildly.

Cal snorted. "One guy arrived about 7 a.m. and got a ride into Bridgeport," he said. "He wanted to resupply. And I hope he wanted a shower. He sure needed one."

Dan asked if the hiker had said anything about the trail conditions.

Cal shook his head. "Not to me…"

Dan gestured over to the trail angels. "Do you know any of them?"

Cal shook his head no.

"A couple of them help us out as volunteers," Dan said. "The big guy, John, over there, for example."

Cal nodded. "From the way he talked, I thought maybe he ran the whole Forest Service."

Dan laughed. "He likes to think so." He pointed to another angel. "The lady in the puffy jacket over there does a ton of stuff for us. Diana."

Cal nodded. "She's the one who brought the coffee."

"That makes sense," Dan said.

Cal stood up. "Well, now that the Forest Service has finally arrived, I can go back down the hill and eat a real breakfast."

Dan stood up, too. "Yeah, I guess it's my turn now. He looked over the newest hiker arrival, an attractive young woman whose legs were shown off in tight black leggings.

Cal glanced at him. "You gonna check her permit?"

Dan shook his head. "Nope. Just gonna ask her if there are any problems on the trail that we should know about."

Cal grinned. "I'd check her permit, anyway. You can never be too careful."

Dan laughed. "Don't eat too much breakfast. You may need to do some digging later today."

Cal shook his head. "Not a chance."

chapter 17

For the next couple of hours, Dan chatted with the trail angels and asked the incoming hikers about the trail. They didn't have much to report. There were some snow patches that required a route around, but those routes were already well established, and nobody was worried about them.

Dan always enjoyed talking to the PCT hikers, even when they seemed more interested in getting a shower and buying pizza. By the time they made it to Sonora Pass, these hikers had a pretty good idea of what they were doing, and had settled into the pace and daily grind of a through-hike. At least they saw him as an ally, rather than an enemy. Sometimes the local backpackers took a different view.

By mid-morning Dan had just about decided that it was time for him to move on when a beat-up old red Ford Bronco pulled into the lot. He knew that vehicle.

Dan walked over to say hello to Travis.

Travis smiled at him and shouted hello over the rough roar of a worn-out muffler.

Dan thought about asking Travis to turn off the engine, but he thought that Travis might just want to keep the old heap running, in case he couldn't get it started again.

Over the noise of the engine, Dan yelled to ask Travis if he was still trying to meet his hiker friend.

Travis nodded and pointed off to the east, yelling that he was going to try to get up to Leavitt Lake.

Dan leaned into the cab of the Bronco and yelled that Travis might want to ask some of the hikers about that guy he wanted to meet.

Travis reached over to turn off the engine and admitted that was a good idea. He reached outside to open the door from the exterior handle. Apparently, this was another area where the Bronco needed a little TLC.

"Are you sure that thing can make it up to Leavitt Lake?" Dan asked.

Travis grinned. "There's a lot of stuff that doesn't work," he said. "But none of that matters. The drivetrain is solid. I've taken it up there a few times before."

Diana called out to say hello to Travis. "Are you here to help us, young man?"

"Sort of," Travis explained. Then he explained how he hoped to meet one of the PCT hikers and give him a ride into Bridgeport.

"That shouldn't be long," Diana replied. "This is pretty much high season for PCT hikers. They're coming through every few minutes or so…"

Travis explained that he was planning to meet one specific hiker.

"That's another story," Diana answered. "Do you know when he's going to get here? Or maybe he's already been and gone?"

Travis pulled out his phone and showed Diana a photo. "This is the guy," Travis said. "Have you seen him?"

Diana shook her head. "I haven't. I haven't been here all the time, but I think most of them are still getting here."

Two hikers trudged down the trail across the highway, and

scrambled across the road into the trail angels' camp. While Dan and Travis watched, the two hikers attacked a table full of drinks and worked their way through three or four cups, grunting their appreciation as they did so.

Dan looked at Travis. "You might want to ask those guys if they've seen your friend on the trail."

The idea didn't seem to appeal to Travis. He held back, just watching the two hikers.

But Diana overheard Dan's comment and called out to Travis. "Where's that photo you showed me?" she said. "Maybe these guys know about him."

Travis pulled out his phone again and handed it to Diana, who showed it to the two hikers. They stared at the photo for a few seconds, then shook their heads and shrugged. "I don't know," one of them muttered.

John arranged for one of the angels to drive the two hikers into Bridgeport. Travis looked at Dan and said that he should probably get going up to Leavitt Lake. He climbed into the Bronco and turned the key. The engine struggled for a minute, then caught with a roar. Travis grinned at Dan.

Just then another hiker trudged into view, a woman with her hair wrapped up tight in a red bandanna. As Travis put his Bronco in gear, Diana met the hiker and waved Travis over.

Travis glanced at Dan. Diana came over and offered to take the phone over to the hiker. She had clearly taken Travis under her wing. She carried the phone over to the new arrival and explained the situation. Dan could see the hiker look at the photo, then start nodding. Behind him, he heard Travis turn off the Bronco. Dan reached for the door handle and let Travis out of the SUV.

The hiker looked over at Travis. "Are you looking for him?"

she asked.

Travis nodded.

"His trail name is Teller. You know, like the magician," she said. "He's the one who doesn't talk."

Travis nodded again. "Yeah, that would be right."

"So, I guess he might be a day behind me," the hiker said. "You can't miss him, because he's got this real old school dark green Kelty pack, and then on top he's rigged this massive solar charger."

Travis nodded again, smiling. "Yeah, that's him."

Dan asked when she had seen him. "We've leapfrogged along, like you do," she said. "I think he tends to hike a little faster, but he also took a big-time break at Tuolumne Meadows. A couple of zero days, at least. But he should be catching up."

Travis thanked her awkwardly, as only a teenage boy can do. Then he turned back to the Bronco, and Dan heard the roar again… slowly moving out of Sonora Pass and heading down the east side of the mountain. Dan could hear the sound of the engine for what seemed like miles.

chapter 18

The next day Dan arrived at the ranger station and was disappointed to see that there were already a few hikers standing in front, waiting in line, and Doris's car pulled in right behind him. He had hoped he would be able to quickly and quietly walk through the entrance and straight into his office in the back.

He unlocked the door, then waited for Doris so that he could let her in as well. Of course she stopped to chat with the hikers, and explain that they would be open right at eight o'clock, and she would get them on their way as quickly as possible.

But once inside the door her manner changed completely.

"Dan, did you hear about that terrible murder over by Big Hill Road?" She could hardly contain herself. "Oh my God, it just sounds awful. Who would do such a thing?"

She stopped and looked at Dan as if she expected him to have an answer.

Dan shook his head in sympathy and mumbled nothing intelligible back to her.

"Have you heard anything from the Sheriff's office?" she asked. "I mean, I hope they find out who did it."

Dan gave her a tight-lipped smile. "I think that first they have to figure out who the victim is," he said. "Apparently that's going to take some time."

"Oh, that is just so awful," Doris said. Dan thought she might actually start crying.

"Why don't you check the phone messages," he said quietly, "and then maybe you can start getting those people out on the trail."

Doris nodded and picked up the phone and started punching buttons. Dan managed to walk back into his office, close the door, and turn on the computer. Before it could boot up, there was a knock on his door.

Doris slowly cracked the door open and said, "There is a message here for you from Steve. He'd like you to call him as soon as you get in."

Dan thanked her and continued to stare at the computer screen. In the back of his mind he was considering the possibility that he might wrap things up early in the office, and then talk Steve into some time off. That way he might be able to hike up and join Kristen for a day or two. And he wondered whether she would think that was nice, or maybe not. Maybe she'd think he was being just a little too creepy. The thought made his stomach churn.

The ring of the phone jolted him back to reality. He picked it up and found Steve Matson on the other end of the line. There wasn't a lot of small talk.

"Dan, I need you to get your report in on that business up in Summit Creek ASAP," he said. "I mean like today at the latest. Before noon would be best." He paused briefly. Dan realized that he would not have to worry about how Kristen would feel about him dropping in on her.

"Nice job up there, by the way," Steve was saying. "Really appreciate the way you managed all of that."

Dan didn't think that he had done much at all, but he kept those thoughts to himself. No need to argue with his boss when his boss was laying it on thick.

"And it looks like we've managed to keep the whole thing down to a dull roar," Steve said. "Those State of Jefferson guys don't know what to do or where to go, so they're just milling around Sonora now, and some of them have already started heading back home."

Dan considered this. Some of them might be leaving, but the really crazy ones were sure to try to do something to get their faces on the news before this blew over. Dan wondered what they would try.

"So listen," Steve was still talking. "Let's see if you can get that report over to me by lunchtime."

Dan grunted a monosyllable of agreement.

But Matson wasn't done. "If you can, I'd like you to be the point man on this other thing with the FBI."

Suddenly he had Dan's full attention.

"You remember your old buddy, Frank Oliver?" Steve continued. "Well, he's back, and he apparently thinks you are the one person in the US Forest Service who knows enough to help him."

Dan gave a dry laugh. "More like the only person he knows up here," he said. "What does he want?"

"You'll have to ask him," Steve said. "Something about trails and hiking between here and Yosemite, but he didn't want to go into any details with me. Those guys are something else."

Dan considered all of this and then took a shot. "So I guess my idea of taking a couple of days off right now isn't going to work out, huh?"

The phone was silent while Steve thought this over. "I don't think there's any way I can make that happen, Dan," he said. "Sorry.

Maybe we can take a look at that next week, after things have settled down a little bit?"

By which time Kristen might well have another job that tied her up every evening.

"So am I supposed to try and call Frank Oliver?" Dan asked.

"He's going to save you that trouble," Steve said. "He's driving up to see you today. Should be there around lunchtime."

Dan gave a slow exhalation of air.

Steve Matson was still talking. "He said this time he would get the sandwiches."

Dan gave another sigh.

"Well, I'll let you get to work on that report," Steve said.

"Yep," Dan replied. "I'll try to crank it out."

He hung up the phone and stared at his computer. There was a good long list of emails awaiting his attention, and Dan resisted the temptation to start opening them. He clicked on the tab to pull up a report form and stared at his screen for a minute.

Doris stuck her head in the door and gave him a questioning look. Dan pointed to his computer and said, "Top priority. They want it by yesterday."

Doris nodded. "I'll let you get to it," she said, and quietly closed the door.

Dan turned to stare at the screen again and then began tapping. After filling in the first two sections of the form, he stopped.

He wondered what kind of sandwich Frank Oliver was going to bring. Then he wondered what Oliver wanted to know.

chapter 19

"Turkey," Frank Oliver said as Dan stared at the sandwich in front of him. "I figured that would be safe."

Dan nodded. He picked it up and started unwrapping it.

"I got chips, too." Oliver passed a bag of corn chips over to Dan.

Dan took a bite out of the sandwich and looked at the FBI agent. He had been surprised to see Oliver show up at his office in what must have passed as hiking clothes in the FBI: Dark green tactical pants, a dark olive-green shirt, and boots that looked like the price sticker was probably still on the sole somewhere. But Oliver still had a slightly hounded look to him, and his pale skin gave him away as someone who didn't spend much time in the sun.

Dan took a swig from the bottle of water Oliver had brought and sat back in his chair. He looked at the FBI agent and waited. He had learned from working with Oliver in the past that it didn't do much good to press him for information.

By the time Dan had eaten most of his sandwich, the FBI agent was ready to talk. Or at least ask questions.

"I thought you might be a good guy to talk to," Oliver began. "We're looking for someone who might be hiking around here."

Dan considered this. "Not a needle in a haystack, but…" he let the sentence trail off. "Is this about those wackos we arrested yesterday?" he asked.

"How close were they to the Pacific Crest Trail?" Oliver asked him.

"A few miles," Dan replied. "There's not a direct trail, but it wouldn't be a long detour."

"Are you sure those guys were really mining?" Oliver asked.

Dan blew out his cheeks. "Who knows?" he said. "They were digging holes in the ground. Tearing up the place. They had rocker boxes and there were piles of tailings. If they weren't mining, they were at least acting like they were mining."

Oliver took this in and then asked, "Did they actually find any gold?"

Dan shook his head. "I doubt it. Maybe enough to convince themselves that they could find more, but it would surprise the hell out of me if they found enough to cover half their expenses, let alone pay themselves anything."

"Do you think it might have been a sham?" Oliver asked.

Dan shook his head. "Miners are strange people. I'm not about to try and guess what they were thinking. All I know is that they dug up a lot of that little canyon and it's going to be a long time before we can make any claim that we've been able to restore it."

He looked over at Frank Oliver. The agent had finished his sandwich and was nursing his bottle of water. Suddenly, Oliver fixed Dan with a stare straight into his eyes. "Question: if someone wanted to disappear for a while, how hard would that be on the Pacific Crest Trail?"

Dan thought this over. "It takes most people five or six months to hike the PCT," he said. "They make stops every ten days or two weeks to get supplies. But if they had a little help, they could stay off the radar for quite a while," he admitted. "You might have a few hikers who would know who he was, or roughly how far along he was, but…" He paused. "And most of them have trail names."

Oliver looked at him quizzically.

"Nobody uses their real name. They get nicknames," Dan explained.

"So, aliases," Oliver suggested.

Dan shrugged.

"We're looking for someone who we think is hiking the PCT," Oliver said. "We're not sure that's what he's doing. He might be faking that, but we can't find him anywhere else." He paused for effect. "And we've been looking."

Dan decided it was time to explain a few things. "Most people generally start at the south end, border of Mexico, in the spring. And they hike north. That's if they're trying to do the whole thing in one shot. Right now, early July, most of the ones who haven't quit are coming through Sonora Pass, or somewhere between Yosemite and Tahoe."

"That's what we were figuring," Oliver said.

"But the trail is 2600 miles long," Dan explained. "Some people leapfrog parts of it. Most people don't hike the whole thing—they bail out at some point."

"And where would they go if they bailed out?" Oliver asked.

"Could be anywhere," Dan replied. "Any road that crosses the PCT is an option. There are lots of those. And you wouldn't have to wait for a road. You could take any number of side trails that would lead you to a road… and bail from there."

Oliver waved his water bottle at Dan and said, "You mean this guy could be anywhere between here and Mexico…"

Dan laughed. "Hell, he could be anywhere at all. Unless you can track him somehow, he could have bailed in the first few hundred miles. That's what most people do. And from there? He could be in Puerto Vallarta on the beach."

"Yeah," Oliver agreed. "But we do have his phone pinging in Tuolumne Meadows about ten days ago."

Dan wondered why he hadn't shared that information before. Then he remembered the last time he had worked with Frank Oliver. Typical.

"That would put him pretty much right on schedule for a through-hike," he said. "If he's still hiking, he could be right around Sonora Pass—or probably a bit north of here now. It all depends on his miles per day."

The two men sat in silence. Then Dan added, "Was that the last cell phone ping you got? Because most people do a resupply at Sonora Pass. It's a good shot from Yosemite to up there, and they don't like to carry more weight than they have to. They'd hike from Tuolumne Meadows to Sonora Pass and then resupply."

Frank Oliver nodded. "That's good. I'll check again, but I think the last cell phone connection was Tuolumne Meadows. And if that's true, then we should get up to Sonora Pass and start looking for this guy."

Dan chuckled. "I don't think I'll be much help," he said. "I don't know who he is, or what he looks like."

Frank Oliver pulled a photo out of a folder and showed it to Dan. "The guy's name is Theo Willyers."

Dan tried to hide his surprise. "Okay. I've heard of him."

"He's one of the wealthiest men in the world," Oliver explained. "And then he just upped and quit his company and started hiking this PCT thing."

Dan thought that this didn't exactly sound like a crime the FBI would be investigating, and he said that to Oliver.

"Except that it looks like he not only walked out on his company to do this," Oliver explained. "He seems to be using this hike as a way of hiding from just about anyone who knows him."

"Still not a crime," Dan said. "Maybe he just needed a break. To reboot."

Frank Oliver gave a sigh and shrugged his shoulders. "No, but when he starts moving money all over the world, that gets the attention of the SEC, for example."

Dan waited. By now he knew that Oliver would continue, if he could stand the suspense. He was right.

"All over the world," Oliver continued. "Including a number of places that we would prefer that large amounts of money not get transferred."

"Foreign countries?" Dan asked, spreading his hands out in confusion.

"And other places."

Dan looked bewildered. "Organizations." Oliver continued. "People that shouldn't be getting support from American citizens."

"Wow," Dan said quietly.

"Okay. Can we head up to Sonora Pass now?" Oliver asked.

Dan nodded. "You know this guy is pretty famous, right?" he said.

"Oh yeah. Regular darling of the computer nerds," Oliver agreed.

"He has a trail name," Dan said. "He goes by Teller on the PCT. And we've talked to a couple of people who might have seen him in the last week or less…"

Frank Oliver stood up. "Good. Let's get up there. Now."

Dan figured he'd better tell him about Travis' plans to help Willyers as a trail angel. The FBI agent listened to the whole story, and then told Dan, "I would give that young man a call and suggest that he find something else to do. If this guy Willyers is dealing with the people we think he is, he is not a nice person. Definitely not someone a kid should be helping in any way."

"Yeah, okay," Dan said. "I'll try giving him a call."

Frank Oliver held his hand up. "Don't try. Make sure that kid doesn't get himself in a mess of trouble. He needs to get out of there and let us catch up with this guy."

As the two men walked out of the ranger station, Dan asked Doris for Travis' number. He felt guilty about not telling her why he wanted it. Once in his vehicle, Dan called the number. As he expected, Travis didn't answer his phone. But he left Travis a pointed message. He hoped it would get through.

chapter 20

Frank Oliver waited while Dan drove ahead of him, leading the way up to Sonora Pass. Dan considered turning on his lights, but then figured that he probably wouldn't get there a lot quicker anyway. There wasn't a lot of traffic on the road, and he drove fast, assuming that Oliver's sedan could keep up.

Dan started running through his options to try and reach Travis. The volunteers at the trailhead might have a phone, but Dan didn't know what number to call. And besides, Travis was a few miles away from them at Leavitt Lake. He could put out an APB on Travis's old Bronco, but chances were it was still up at the lake, and nobody would see it. And if anyone were to put out an APB, it should be Frank Oliver and the FBI, not Dan.

He wondered if Cal might still be up at the pass. Once he hit a straight section of highway, he hit Cal's number on his phone.

Cal answered quickly." What's up, Dan?"

Dan asked him if he'd seen Travis.

"Nah, I don't think so. It's been pretty quiet up here." Cal said. "I ran down to Kennedy Meadows for a while to see how they're doing with the roadblock there. That's pretty quiet, too. I guess the State of Jefferson guys are back down in Sonora or something."

Dan got right to the point. "Listen, Cal. Travis is up at Leavitt

Lake trying to meet some guy on the PCT. Only it turns out the guy he's trying meet is in big trouble. Is there any chance I could talk you into driving up there and pulling him out of there?"

For a moment, Dan thought that he had lost the phone connection. "Shit," he heard Cal say. "You want me to leave my oil pan somewhere up there on that road?"

"Travis was driving that in his old Bronco," Dan pointed out.

Another long pause. "So where exactly is Travis?" Cal finally asked. "Is he just hanging out at the lake?"

"No, he was planning to hike up to the PCT to meet this guy." Dan thought about that for a minute. It wasn't going to make Cal happy.

"So am I supposed to drive up there and then drag my ass up to the PCT?" Cal asked. He didn't sound pleased at all.

"Look," Dan explained. "Just drive up to the lake and see if Travis' Bronco is there. If it is, he'll have to come back to the Bronco to get out of there, and you can take over from there. Just get Travis away from that guy if he's with him."

Dan waited for a response, then realized that the connection had gone dead. He had no idea if Cal had heard that last part of the conversation. He tried calling back, but he no longer had cell phone service. He put his phone away.

That hadn't gone well at all. Now he had about thirty minutes to think about it before he could get to Sonora Pass.

As he neared Kennedy Meadows, he heard Frank Oliver honk his horn and flash his lights. Dan pulled over and Frank Oliver pulled alongside. Through his open window, Oliver shouted, "One of us ought to get up to the pass right away."

"But my radio isn't working up here, and we should get the word out to all the LEO in the area. Can you stop at the roadblock here and take care of that? You've got a good description of this guy and all?"

Dan nodded. Of course, Oliver wanted to be up at the pass, so that he could make the arrest if the guy showed up.

Dan explained that he had asked Cal to run up to the lake.

"Shit, you mean there is no LEO at the pass right now?" Oliver asked.

Dan nodded again.

"See you in a few minutes," Oliver said. "And get some back-up sent up there ASAP." Then he roared off up the road.

Dan drove up to Kennedy Meadows and up to the roadblock. He recognized Ruben Arriaga, a young deputy with the Sheriff's office. Ruben walked over and Dan got out of his vehicle.

The two men shook hands and Dan noticed that his own hand was sweaty.

He quickly ran through the information: The car that just drove by was an FBI agent. Arriaga should call his dispatch and get information about a guy by the name of Theo Willyers from the FBI. Keep a sharp lookout for him up here. And send available units to Sonora Pass. The young Sheriff's attitude went from calm and friendly to all business as Dan explained the situation.

Ruben got on his radio and called in. Dan waited just long enough to make sure that the communication was going through, then climbed into his vehicle and pulled back out onto the highway. Sonora Pass was only a few minutes away, but it was a twisty few miles to get there.

He drove as fast as he dared.

By the time he got to Sonora Pass, Frank Oliver was sitting in a chair, having a cup of coffee.

Dan explained that he was going to drive up to Leavitt Lake to help Cal look for Travis.

Oliver nodded his agreement. "You get Travis the hell out of there," he said. "If you got that message through, I should have back-up here pretty soon."

Dan looked around at the trail angels, who were observing the two men with considerable interest. "Do you want to evacuate these people?" he asked.

Oliver considered this. "This guy is white collar. No evidence that he is armed. I also don't want to have him get scared and take off hiking back up the trail. He's way better set up for that than we are. If I see him, I'll ask these people to leave him to me. And I'll have a couple of back-up here in a few minutes."

"Do you want me to wait?" Dan asked.

Oliver shook his head. "Go get that kid out of there."

Dan checked his watch. It was just past two o'clock, and the weather report for this afternoon called for some thundershowers. He looked at the sky and had to admit that the weather report might well be accurate. That should make the drive up to the lake just a little more exciting.

He drove down a few miles to the turn-off and then eased his SUV onto the rough road. Like many of these old roads, there were stretches that were absolutely awful, and some of the rest of it was pretty good. The secret was in knowing which was which. Dan gently guided his SUV over the first few massive potholes, then sped up as the road improved. It was only two miles, he told himself. But it was the last mile that was the most brutal…

chapter 21

When he arrived at the lake, he saw Cal's vehicle at the top of the road. There was no sign of the red Bronco. Dan drove over to the Sheriff's car and pulled alongside.

"No sign of Travis?" he asked.

Cal shook his head. "No Travis, no red Bronco. The kid probably got tired of waiting and went home."

Dan looked around. "Well, he's not here. That's good."

Cal grinned. "You could hike up to the PCT from here while I wait," he suggested. "You can never be too careful, you know."

"Nope," Dan responded. "If the Bronco isn't here, Travis isn't here. That's good enough for me."

Cal got out of his car and walked over to lean on the roof of Dan's SUV.

"Unless he's already with your pal Willyers," Cal said. "In which case they are together and could be just about anywhere right now."

"Did you ask anybody up here about the Bronco?" Dan asked, waving a hand at the few fishermen who dotted the lake.

"The guy over there remembers seeing the Bronco, and it left a couple of hours ago," Cal said.

"Did he see how many people were in it?" Dan asked.

Cal shook his head. "Nope. I think at this point we put out an alert for that Bronco. If we find Travis parked up some side road with his girlfriend, that would be really great news."

Dan agreed. "Reach out for the CHP and see if they have a unit in Bridgeport. That's where they would go if this guy is getting a resupply."

Cal nodded and walked back around to his vehicle to make the call. Dan listened in as Cal got on the radio. When he was done, Cal looked over at Dan.

"Nice quiet week we're having around here, huh?" Cal said. "You go off to fight with the Marines, we got the State of Jefferson in open rebellion, and now we're supposed to be looking for dangerous hikers on the PCT… and maybe a kid in a Bronco."

Dan looked at him. "Not my idea of fun."

"Oh yeah," Cal replied. "You want to wander in the woods. Hey, have I told you the latest about the body they found in that old mine?" he asked Dan.

Dan chuckled. "I bet that I know less about that than just about anyone else in Tuolumne County." He paused. When Cal gave him a questioning look, Dan explained. "From what I heard from my neighbors last night, everybody knows all about it, and everybody's got a theory about it."

Cal gave a derisive snort. "Body burned, no ID, no prints, pretty darn clean crime scene. That's one that's going to take some work. But the latest is they think it may be some kind of foreign spy deal. Lots of Feds involved."

"But you're up here enjoying the view of the lake," Dan said.

"Only because a friend of mine asked for a favor," Cal replied.

"What I read in the paper is that the body was burned pretty badly," Dan said. "So I am going to assume that means that somebody was trying to hide the identity of the victim." Dan paused. "It wasn't just burned by accident?"

Cal shook his head, and then added, "A very professional job. We don't get a lot of those up here. We get mainly amateurs."

Dan considered this for a minute. As a ranger, he wasn't really involved much in the major crimes in Tuolumne County. That was Cal's job.

"So what does that mean?" he asked. "Drugs? That's about all I can think of up here that might attract that kind of attention. Or did they just decide that this was a nice place to dump a body, far from the scene of the crime?"

"Exactly," Cal said.

A gust of wind blew down from the peaks and sent a chill over the two men. Dan heard the noise of a truck starting up and noticed that some of the fishermen were moving towards the parking area. Dark clouds were gathering among the surrounding peaks.

"Let's get out of here," Dan said.

"I'd offer to race you down," Cal said. "But not on this road."

The two SUVs slowly bumped out of the clearing and carefully rocked and rolled down the road.

chapter 22

By the time they got back to Sonora Pass, the clouds were covering most of the sky. The team of trail angels were taking cover inside a small RV parked off to the side of the parking lot. Up above, on the trail, Dan could see a single hiker trudging downhill.

"She'll want a warm shower tonight," he heard one of the women in the RV say.

Dan noticed Frank Oliver was sitting in his car. As he got closer, he noticed the engine running. Dan glanced up at the sky as he walked over to talk to the FBI agent.

"Did you find him?" Oliver asked, with raised eyebrows.

Dan shook his head.

"I didn't think so," Oliver said.

"I'm hoping that he gave up and headed home," Dan replied.

Oliver nodded. "Well, the good news is that he doesn't have to worry about waiting for Mr. Willyers anymore," he added.

Dan shot him a questioning look.

"Theo Willyers is not hiking the PC Trail, or any other trail. At least not anymore," Oliver continued.

"Are you sure about that?" Dan asked him.

"Oh, I'm sure," Oliver said. "He's dead. And he's been dead for about five days or so."

"What?" The look on Dan's face asked a fistful of questions.

Frank Oliver nodded again. "Turns out that body they found down in that old mine is none other than Mr. Theo Willyers. RIP."

"Are you sure?" Dan asked. "I mean, it was badly burned and all…"

"Theo Willyers had an ID chip in his neck," Oliver explained. "Once our forensic team got a look at the body, there was no question. Apparently, the local coroner missed that…" Oliver never quite seemed to lose a slightly condescending tone when he talked.

Over his shoulder, Dan noticed Cal's SUV pull into the parking lot.

Dan turned to stare up at the trail on the south side of the pass. He heard Cal's SUV come to a stop and the engine shut off.

Frank Oliver motioned for Dan to lean in closer. "This guy Willyers has a huge amount of stock," he said. "Major financial implications. Better not say anything to anyone. I probably shouldn't have said anything to you… the SEC is watching, and his company is going to want to manage the news."

Dan nodded. He wasn't exactly fond of talking to anyone from the news media anyway. Not that he had done it very often. But when he had, it usually didn't turn out quite the way he expected.

He heard Cal's door open and turned to greet him.

"That includes your friendly local sheriff," he heard Oliver say behind him.

Dan gave a thumbs up to the voice behind him as he walked over to meet Cal.

But before he could reach Cal a voice called out from the RV.

"Hey, guys, Clarabelle here says she saw Teller on the trail just yesterday."

Dan turned towards the RV to see who was calling out to him. Diana was waving to him.

As her words sank into Dan's mind, he turned and motioned to Frank Oliver. The FBI agent had been on the point of leaving.

The hiker, a young woman who was covered from head to toe in black, and was wearing an enormous pair of sunglasses, came out of the RV and walked up to Dan. Her face, tanned and streaked with dirt, was only a couple of shades paler than her clothes. "Are you looking for Teller?" she asked. "He was at Dorothy Lake yesterday. He should be along pretty soon, if he wasn't already ahead of me."

Dan looked at her carefully. He was trying to decide how much credence he should give to her report. One of the first classes he ever took in law enforcement addressed the unreliability of eyewitnesses. Frank Oliver got out of his car, and Dan explained the situation to him.

"She says she saw him yesterday," Dan said.

"Well, she didn't," Oliver replied.

Dan asked Clarabelle if she was sure it was Teller.

"Hell yeah," she said. "Nobody else is hiking with a thirty-year-old Kelty pack and stack of solar chargers on top. It was him."

Dan asked her if she had a photo of Teller.

The young woman thought about this for a minute, and then explained that the photo she had wouldn't do them much good. "It was taken on our first night out. We all look pretty different now. But the pack and rig are the same. You can't miss those. Especially his."

Dan turned to look at Frank Oliver.

"Somebody want to tell me what's going on?" he heard Cal say.

Frank Oliver turned around and climbed into his car and slammed the door shut. Dan could see him pull out a radio and start talking.

Cal looked at Dan and opened his hands up in front of his belt. "So?"

Dan shook his head. "So somebody is either dead, or not dead and is hiking the PCT," he said. "Or Teller is not Willyers. Or… something else. And right now, your guess is as good as mine."

Dan's radio crackled on. Doris had some information for him.

"Dan, I heard that bulletin looking for Travis's old Bronco. I know where it is," Doris was saying.

Dan answered his radio. "Okay, so where is he?"

"Well, I don't exactly know where he is," Doris explained. "But I know where he was."

Dan sighed and waited for Doris to get to the point.

"It's on his Facebook page," she continued." "Travis posted on his Facebook page that he had met his friend Theo and taken him into Bridgeport to resupply earlier today. He even has a photo."

Dan and Cal exchanged looks. "Doris, are you saying that Travis has a photo of this guy Willyers?"

"They were in Bridgeport together earlier today," she said. "So you can stop worrying about him."

From inside the car, Dan heard Frank Oliver say "Shit!"

<h1 style="text-align:center">chapter 23</h1>

Dan and Cal stood silently while they watched FBI agent Frank Oliver wave his hands inside the car as he talked on the radio. They could see the tension and anger in his body as the conversation continued.

"I'll call in another note about Travis' Bronco," he said. "CHP might have a car down in Bridgeport and they can do a quick check. It's not like there are a lot of places to hide in Bridgeport."

Dan looked over at the trail angel's RV. "We got any hikers in there?" he asked. "Maybe we should see if they know anything."

Clarabelle was about to get into a car for a ride into Bridgeport. Dan called out to her, "Can we ask you just a few more questions?"

She didn't look pleased at the prospect, but gave a shrug and then nodded.

Cal looked at Dan. "What are we looking for, exactly?" he asked.

Dan took a deep breath and let it out slowly. "I guess we need to find out exactly where this guy Teller is. The one that doesn't talk. Where did she see him, how fast was he hiking? Was he with anyone else?" Dan let his voice trail off. Then he added, "Did she see him carrying any weapons?"

"Great," Cal said. "This is going to be fun…"

Dan walked over to the RV and asked if anyone there could

add any information about Teller. Diana explained that they had never seen him, but that they had asked all the hikers today. None of them knew much about him, or had seen him quite a few days ago. "Seems like Tuolumne Meadows was where a lot of people saw him. Maybe he didn't make it here yet," she suggested. "He could come tomorrow."

"Yeah," Dan said. But he knew that Travis had intercepted the hiker at Leavitt Lake, and taken him into Bridgeport.

When Frank Oliver got out of his car, he walked over to Dan. "We're looking for the kid's Bronco right now," he said. "If it's in Bridgeport, we'll find it."

Dan nodded. "Doris said that Travis posted that picture earlier today. He could still be there, but he could also be hours away…"

Dan spied another hiker working down the trail to the pass. He pointed with his chin. "Here's another one."

Oliver asked Dan if he had questioned the volunteers in the RV.

"Yep. They've been asking people about this guy Teller, but apparently Clarabelle there is the only one who really made a connection. Couple of other people have seen the guy, but they can't remember when, or it was days ago."

He looked at Frank Oliver. "You can go ask them yourself if you want. I might have missed something."

Oliver shook his head, then looked down at the ground.

"The thing is, we're pretty sure that the body is Theo Willyers," he said quietly. "And I've just found out that somebody made a bunch of money and stock transactions today. And the phone pinged a tower in Bridgeport."

Dan took this in. "So shouldn't we get down there?"

Frank Oliver looked at him. "We have enough people down there," he said. "My job is to stay here and keep my eyes open."

"You're not running this investigation?" Dan asked. He immediately regretted having said it.

Oliver snorted. "Hell, no. This is way over my pay grade. My job was to check out the trail thing. We have quite a few agents in on this. And I'm just a lowly worker ant."

Dan was thinking. "So, if this guy made it to Bridgeport, which it looks like he did, and that was a couple of hours ago or more, he could be headed for LA, or Reno… Salt Lake City. And that's assuming that we know who he is."

Dan paused. Off in the distance, Dan heard the slow rumble of thunder.

"Do we know who he is?" Dan asked.

Frank Oliver didn't answer right away. He sucked on his cheek for a minute. "Maybe," he said. "We may not know exactly who he is, but we think we might know who some of his friends are."

Dan looked at him and raised his eyebrows.

"Bad guys," Oliver said. "His friends are bad guys."

Cal walked over to them. "This guy says he saw Teller two days ago. Says he was hiking slower than usual. But he may have been looking for a lunch stop or something… That would put him somewhere near here today. But we already know that, I guess?"

Cal looked at the FBI agent. "Do you want to tell us what the hell is going on?" he asked.

Oliver took a moment to reply. Dan could tell he was conflicted about telling them what he knew. "We know that the body in that old mine is Theo Willyers," Oliver started. "At least, that's the assumption we're working with. That's what the computer chip says."

"So who is this guy on the trail?" Cal asked.

Oliver shrugged. "It looks like he has Willyers' gear. So that is very suspicious."

"So maybe he had something to do with Willyers' death," Cal added.

"Or with the people who killed him," Oliver said. "That is my assumption. Yes."

Dan and Cal exchanged a look, and Oliver noticed it.

"Okay," he said. "Willyers is worth multi-billions. And right now, some of those billions are getting moved to accounts in Russia, and other places." He paused. "This is absolutely classified stuff." He looked around to make sure that Dan and Cal understood. And that nobody else could hear them.

They both nodded.

"One theory is that some pretty sophisticated criminals are involved. Somehow they got to Willyers, and it looks like they now have access to his accounts."

"Well," Cal said. "They beat the crap out of him and then killed him."

"That's what we think," Oliver said. "They beat the crap out of him to get his security codes and his phone. And right now, this guy hiking the PCT may be pretending to be Theo Willyers. And moving his money around on the side."

"But if he's dead, aren't his accounts frozen?" Dan asked.

Oliver nodded. "Yeah, we're on that. But in the meantime, they are sending huge amounts of money around. And Willyers' company is freaking out. He's the whole company, founder, visionary, leader. . . everything. Without him, the whole thing could implode. So they are being…cautious about what they say. And what they will allow us to say."

"Even to a bank?"

Oliver blew out a puff of air. "Forget the banks. That's small stuff. It's the SEC that's worried."

"Shit," Cal said. "This stuff is beyond me. Why not just announce he's dead?"

"That's in the works," Oliver said. "At least, as far as I know. But once we do that, the bad guys know that we know."

"Well, yeah, but the money train stops," Cal said. "Doesn't it?"

"Eventually. Like I said," Oliver reminded him, "it's in the works. But Theo Willyers has a long history of doing crazy things."

"So everybody wants to make sure," Dan suggested.

Oliver nodded. "And meanwhile, he keeps hiking the PCT. Or somebody pretending to be him does. Which is sure as hell confusing the issue. All the issues."

"Good place to hide, if people think you are dead," Cal said.

"Exactly," Oliver replied. "And somewhere, this guy is going to meet somebody else. We'd like to know who that is."

"Do you have any leads on that?" Dan asked.

Oliver nodded. "We're watching a few people."

A car slowly pulled into the parking lot and drove over to the RV. The driver, an older, bearded man wearing a plaid shirt and zip-off pants, hopped out and started carrying boxes into the RV.

"Another volunteer," Dan explained. "He works our counter sometimes. His wife makes good cookies."

The man came back out of the RV and trotted over to Dan. "I hear you guys are looking for an old red Ford Bronco?" he said. "I used to have one of those. A real POS."

The three men drew closer as Dan assured him they were looking for that Bronco.

"It's down at the St. Mary's Pass trailhead," he said. "I stopped in there on my way up here, and it's parked up under some trees down there."

Dan, Cal and Frank Oliver all turned to get into their cars. As Dan started his engine, he noticed the first drops of rain on his windshield.

<h1 style="text-align:center">chapter 24</h1>

Dan was the first car out of the parking lot, but Cal and Frank Oliver were not far behind in theirs. They all immediately found themselves behind a large, slow RV. Dan considered turning on his lights and siren, but they were only going another mile. He decided against it.

Cal wasn't so patient. As Dan heard the siren behind him, he waited for the RV to pull over, then sped past. In less than a minute he was pulling onto the rough dirt road that served as the parking area for the trailhead.

Sure enough, up in one corner, underneath a large juniper tree, sat Travis' tired old Bronco. Dan parked his vehicle and walked over to the Bronco. Travis was not inside. He looked on the ground. It looked like two sets of footprints got out of the Bronco and headed towards the trailhead. One set of footprints could have been about the size of Travis' feet.

Cal and Frank Oliver joined him.

"I've called this in to my office," Oliver said. "We should be getting some additional officers here pretty soon."

Dan looked at him. "I don't think that I am willing to wait until they get here," he said. "If this kid is in danger, I'm going after him right now. Every minute means they are getting farther away. And it's getting late."

Oliver looked at Cal, who nodded. "I'm in," the Sheriff volunteered.

The FBI agent took a deep breath. "Okay," he said. He looked at Cal. "Are you carrying a firearm?"

Cal pointed to the pistol in the holster on his belt.

Frank Oliver looked at Dan, who shook his head. Cal immediately went to his vehicle and pulled out the shotgun from the dash. He handed it to Dan with a handful of shells. "Try not to shoot anyone on our side with this," he said. "And it's probably better if you let us go first…"

Dan took the shotgun and put the shells into his shirt pocket. By then, Frank Oliver had already started up the trail. Cal turned to hike after him, leaving Dan behind him.

They hadn't gone two hundred yards when Oliver paused on the trail. As Dan reached him, he realized that the FBI agent was panting heavily and out of breath. Cal, with his bad knee, was limping along as well.

Dan didn't stop. He hiked past the other two men and kept moving up the trail, long strides keeping a steady pace that quickly left the other two men behind. They would have to catch up when and if they could.

The trail switch backed up the side of the pass, occasionally coming out into the open, but often going through tunnels of high brush that reached over Dan's head. Dan was pushing hard, his blood pumping both with the exertion and the sense of panic he was fighting.

At one point, Dan came out into a field of mule ears not quite yet in full bloom, and looked back to see both Cal and Frank Oliver well back on the trail. He could see the top of the pass, but in between the trail was hidden.

Dan was really pushing himself now. He was taking deep breaths with every two steps, hiking with rhythm, and forcing himself to keep up the pace. He knew he couldn't last forever at this rate, but if he could get to the top of the pass, less than two miles ahead, the rest of the trail was downhill and much easier. His shirt was now beginning to stick to his back as he became over-heated and started to sweat.

At the same time, it felt good to be doing something, anything. The shotgun was a nuisance, but Dan carried it over his shoulder like a shovel, trying to find a balanced position for it. His breathing was more labored now, and he slacked off his pace just a touch, still moving forward as best he could.

The next tunnel of brush was in front of him, and he was so focused on his hiking that he almost ran into a hiker coming the other direction. As he started in surprise and then began to push past the oncoming hiker, Dan realized it was Doris' grandson Travis.

"Hey," Travis said. "How ya doin'?"

Dan struggled to get his breath. He pointed his finger at Travis and said, "Good to see you here." He gasped again. "We were worried about you."

Travis gave him a puzzled look.

"You okay?" Dan gasped out.

Travis shrugged. "Yeah, why?"

"Did you meet that guy you were looking for?" Dan asked. "The computer guy?"

Travis shook his head. "Nah," he said disgustedly. He paused for a minute, clearly trying to come up with the words he needed. "I mean, I met a guy who looked like him, but it wasn't him."

Dan nodded. "Okay," he said. "And you're okay?"

Travis laughed uncomfortably. "Yeah, I'm fine. What's the big deal?" His eyes suddenly took in the shotgun on Dan's shoulder.

Dan shook his head. "It's okay," he said. "We were afraid something might have happened to you."

By this time Dan could see Frank and Cal coming into view along the trail behind him. He waved to them and pointed to Travis.

Cal gave him a thumbs-up sign, and immediately stopped hiking. Frank Oliver struggled on for a few steps, then stopped as well.

"Come on," Dan said to Travis. "Let's go tell them the good news."

chapter 25

Travis and Dan hiked back down to where Cal and Frank Oliver were now sitting on the side of the trail.

"Hey buddy," Cal said as a greeting. "Good to see you."

"Yeah, I guess," Travis said. "Sorry if I did something to make you worried." He looked from one to the other of the men, hoping to get some kind of explanation.

"Travis said that he met someone who looked like what's-his-name the computer guy, but it wasn't him," Dan explained to the others.

"What do you mean?" Oliver asked. He looked at Travis. "Tell me exactly what happened."

"It wasn't him," Travis said. "It was just some random guy on the trail."

Frank Oliver shook his head. "No, I mean it. Tell me exactly what happened. From the minute you met this guy."

Travis gave a little shrug. "Okay." He clearly couldn't see why the men were so focused, but he gave it a shot.

"I was up at Leavitt Lake, and I saw a guy that looked like Theo Willyers," he said. "So that's who I was waiting for."

Dan nodded.

"How did you know it was him?" Oliver asked.

"Oh, you know… I'd seen photos," Travis said. "And his pack

was pretty radical, so there was that."

"How so?" Oliver asked.

"It was an old dark green Kelty external frame pack," Travis said. "Nobody uses those anymore. It was from his college days. And a big set of solar panels on top."

Oliver nodded. "Okay, so that's what this guy had?"

"Oh, yeah," Travis said. "I was sure it was him. And he wasn't talking, so that part made sense, too."

"He was supposed to be hiking the PCT in silence," Dan explained. "That was part of the deal."

"So did you ask him who he was?" Oliver asked Travis.

"Well, er, no," the young man stumbled. "I mean, he didn't want to be recognized…. and the silence thing… I figured he wouldn't say anything anyway."

Frank Oliver followed up. "So after you met him…where did you meet him? And then what happened?"

"Okay. This was on the trail above Leavitt Lake," Travis said. "I was parked there, and when I saw that pack, I figured I'd go up and meet him on the trail. So that's what I did. And then I just said that I was there to give him a ride into town, if that's what he wanted. To Bridgeport."

"And he said yes?" Oliver asked.

"Well… he nodded," Travis said. "And so I figured fine…and so we went back to the Bronco and I gave him a ride into Bridgeport."

Frank Oliver nodded. "Okay, this is important, Travis. What did he do in Bridgeport?"

Travis shrugged his shoulders. "Not much. Went to the store and bought a bunch of food… grabbed some lunch at that Mexican place. They had free Wi-Fi…I mean, so we didn't talk. He did some stuff on his phone, and I did, too."

"Good," said Oliver. "And how much food did he buy? Did he buy anything else?"

Again, Travis shrugged. "I don't know. Some oatmeal, a salami. Some ramen. Not a lot." He paused. "But you guys know it wasn't Willyers, right? It was someone else?"

Frank Oliver looked at Travis carefully. "And how do you know that?" he asked.

Travis snorted. "Because when he bought stuff, he didn't use his phone or his app. He paid cash. And he couldn't figure out the Wi-Fi. I had to help him."

The three older men looked at him in confusion.

"Geez, guys," Travis said. "Theo Willyers was like a revolutionary. He totally changed smart phones. He always said that with Allapp, you never needed anything else. But this guy was clueless. He didn't even know how to use his phone for stuff. I had to show him how to share a photo."

Frank Oliver sat back and folded his arms. "Got it. He had a pack just like Willyers. And you say he looked like Willyers?" He paused.

Travis nodded. "I mean, after like a bunch of weeks on the PCT, I guess," Travis said.

"Right," Oliver agreed. "But it wasn't Willyers." Here he looked intently at Travis.

"I don't think so," Travis said, shaking his head dismissively.

"And he didn't speak, is that right?" Oliver asked Travis.

Travis shook his head.

"Not even in a phone call?"

"No… he was like texting or something, but not a phone call," Travis explained.

"Think carefully," Oliver said to Travis. "Did you see a firearm?

Anything else that you might have noticed?"

Travis shook his head. "I mean, I didn't look in his pack or anything. And he put that food in there while I was taking a leak. He seemed like a normal guy, I guess… he smelled bad, and I was a little surprised that he wasn't going to take a night off and get clean."

Frank Oliver gave a deep sigh. The three men had finally got their breath back. "My guess is that he didn't want to stay in one place that long," Oliver said. "So then what happened?"

"So then I asked him if he had a place to stay, and he just pointed to his pack and the mountains," Travis said. "So I asked him if he wanted a ride back up again, and he nodded."

Dan interrupted. "But you didn't take him back to the trailhead at Leavitt Lake, or Sonora Pass?"

"That was my idea," Travis explained. "I told him there were a bunch of people at Sonora Pass, and that he could start here and still hit the trail without dealing with all of that."

A light rain shower started falling on the four men as they stood on the trail.

"But then?" Cal asked. "Looks like you wanted to join him for part of the hike…"

"Well, not exactly," Travis said. "But by the time we got here, I was pretty sure this guy wasn't Theo Willyers. But I knew he might not be able to figure out how to get to the PCT from here, so I hiked to the top of the pass to show him."

"And is that all?" Dan asked.

"Well," Travis added, "I just figured I'd tag along while he hiked a bit, to see if I could figure out what was going on. And why he was doing this."

Frank Oliver raised his eyebrows. "And did you?"

Travis shook his head. "Nah. I got as far as the pass and told him to have a good hike. Then I came back here."

Oliver looked at Dan and Cal. "That's probably a really, really good thing," he said.

chapter 26

The light rain was now becoming steady, and the wind was gusting through the nearby trees. Dan checked the sky to the west, where dark clouds were forming in lowering banks. He pulled his rainshell out of his daypack and put it on. The other two men didn't seem to have a similar solution.

They sent Travis down the trail to the trailhead. Frank Oliver asked him to wait for a couple of agents who were on their way from Sonora so that Travis could tell those agents everything he knew.

"You mean, what I just told you guys?" Travis asked.

"Yep," Oliver replied. "And anything else you might remember on the way back down."

Travis nodded, and then glanced at Dan. It looked to Dan like he wanted to ask a question, but instead, the young man turned and started hiking down the trail.

Dan looked up at the sky. The clouds were closing in.

He turned to Frank Oliver. "Are you ready to keep hiking?" he asked. "I think we can still catch this guy."

Oliver looked dubious. His jacket was starting to look pretty wet. "I think it is better to wait for our back-up." He looked up at the sky. "There's some clear sky over there," he said, pointing to the east.

"Weather comes from this side," Dan said, pushing his chin out to the west. The sky there was somewhere between gray and black.

"Well, I am not going to outrun this guy anyway," Cal said, interrupting their weather analysis. "If you want, I can wait for the back-up down at the trailhead. That's if you guys want to go on."

Oliver still looked dubious. It was clear to Dan that the FBI agent didn't relish the idea of racing up over the pass. But Dan wasn't going to wait.

"There are some more people on the other side of this pass," Dan said. "A group of scientists. I know someone with them." He glanced at Cal, who nodded.

Oliver nodded. "Okay…"

"I am going to go after this guy, and hopefully catch him before he gets to them," Dan said. He reached into his pack and handed the FBI agent a cheap rain poncho. "This might help. In case the rain gets worse."

"Okay," Oliver agreed. "I'll go." Then he turned to Cal. "Any chance we can get some support up here?" he asked. "How long will it take a chopper to get here?"

Cal shook his head. "Not in this weather." By now the clouds were lowering so that the top of the pass was shrouded in mist. "They wouldn't be able to see anything anyway."

Oliver nodded, then turned to Dan. "Let's go. You lead the way."

But Dan had already started hiking.

chapter 27

After calling in a quick report to dispatch, Dan put his radio away. He had a long list of questions to ask the FBI agent as they hiked, but he knew that every breath Oliver spent on answering a question would slow him down on the hike. Better to leave it all unsaid, and hike as hard as possible.

But he did wonder. If this involved Russia, did it also involve the CIA? What about the SEC that Oliver had mentioned? Who watches their back? And if these were Russian criminals they were chasing, didn't the FBI keep tabs on these guys? If they knew they were Russians, didn't they know more than that? Like names and addresses? Photos?

And at the same time, Dan had more personal concerns. Kristen and her group were just a few miles down into a canyon on the other side of the pass. And that could put her directly into harm's way. If this guy headed down that canyon, he would run right into their camp. And if he was as bad a character as the FBI seemed to think, that meant real danger to the whole group.

Dan started to hike faster, then realized he was leaving Frank Oliver behind. He stopped for a minute to let the agent catch up. He had to hand it to Oliver. For someone who was twenty years older, and lived at sea level, the guy was making every effort to hurry. When Oliver caught up to Dan, Dan asked him if he wanted a short rest. Oliver didn't answer. He just pointed up the trail and, gasping for breath, motioned for Dan to keep going.

At the top of the pass the visibility was less than a hundred yards. A combination rain and mist had soaked everything, and Dan was still hearing distant thunder to the north. That was where they were headed, although the thunder was miles away, if Dan was estimating correctly.

Dan pointed off to his right. "We need to work our way over that ridge," he said to Frank Oliver. "That's where we pick up the PCT from here."

The FBI agent didn't look pleased, but he nodded in agreement.

The rough use trail led them along a contour until it dropped down into the canyon of the East Carson River.

Dan suddenly wondered where Captain Lewis and his Marines were. They would be a help right now. But they were probably back down at the base, telling stories about their adventure.

A gust of wind caught Dan's hat and blew it off his head. That didn't happen very often, and it got his attention. The storm was clearly getting worse. He chased it down and put it away in his pack. The rainshell hood would have to do.

They had begun to drop down now, below the clouds, and Dan could see down the valley. They were only a mile from the nearest grove of trees, and further down, the whole valley was carpeted with forest.

Dan knew that deeper in the canyon a steep waterfall isolated the upper canyon from the rest of the river. That was what allowed the upper canyon to hold a small population of native Piute trout. So Kristen's camp would be above the falls. But from here, Dan couldn't see where that would be. There was a side canyon coming in from the west a few miles down. Maybe that was where they would camp.

The trail was pretty minimal, just a track through the grass and brush that sometimes looked like a game trail. From time to time, Dan had to choose between one trail and another. He wasn't really sure it made any difference, since they all led downhill, down into the canyon.

He strained his eyes to look through the rain, but he couldn't see anything that looked like a tent, or a camp. And he couldn't see another hiker.

That was the bad news. The good news was that there didn't seem to be any place for a Russian criminal to hide and ambush them. The thought gave Dan a small amount of comfort. It would be different once they got into the trees. If the Russian knew he was being followed...

Lots of ifs, Dan thought.

A crack of thunder on the peak above sent a shot of adrenaline through him. That one was close. And before he had a chance to pull himself together, another crack just down the canyon shattered the air.

Dan quickly looked back for Frank Oliver. The FBI agent had pulled his poncho over his head and was trying to hold it together against the wind and rain. He didn't look happy. But he was still hiking downhill.

Dan waited for him to catch up again. A blast of wind came through, followed by a torrent of rain. Dan held onto the hood of his poncho with one hand and turned his head away from the rain. He didn't realize that Oliver was close until he heard the agent's voice call out.

"Well, this sucks." It wasn't said with anger, just a recognition of the facts.

A third crack of thunder, seemingly right overhead, sent both men ducking and running downhill. The trail was now just a blur. Maybe they were on it, maybe not. But it was imperative that they get to lower ground.

A small bend in the canyon showed them some bushes tucked into the hillside.

Dan pointed them out. "Let's get down there and see if we can find a little shelter!" he yelled at Oliver. He didn't wait for an answer. He just turned and continued to slosh his way through the rain. Despite his jacket, he was soaked from the thighs down. He assumed Oliver was in much worse shape.

There were two more thunderous claps before they made it into a small cluster of alders above the creek. A rock overhang on the western side gave them a tiny ledge of shelter from the worst of the wind and rain, but it was far from an ideal location.

As Frank Oliver climbed into the bushes next to him, Dan pulled out a flimsy mylar emergency blanket and tried to fashion it into a cover over their heads. He was only moderately successful.

The two men sat huddled close together underneath the mylar, watching the rain pour down.

Frank Oliver looked over at Dan and repeated, "This sucks."

And that's when it started to hail.

chapter 28

At first Dan thought it was beginning to snow, as the rain became less transparent. Then he felt the stinging on his hands and realized it was hail.

Another clap of thunder came, deafeningly close.

Dan turned and glanced at Frank Oliver, huddling next to him. The FBI agent didn't look good. Dan noticed that he seemed to be shivering slightly, and the color of his face was closer to blue than pink.

"You doing okay?" he asked.

Oliver nodded, making only brief eye contact with Dan.

Dan had slipped his pack off his shoulders and tucked it in between his legs as they sat on the side of the hill. He reached into one of the side pockets and pulled out an energy bar.

"Here," he said. "Eat this. It'll make you feel better."

The FBI agent took the bar without saying anything, tore it open, and took a big bite.

Dan took a quick look around. The bend in the canyon came where a small dry drainage fed into the river. But now that drainage was a regular creek, adding the noise of its rushing water to the cacophony of sound around them.

"Thanks," he heard Frank Oliver say, his mouth still full of the energy bar.

Dan waved his hand, to brush off the comment.

"Comes with the territory," he said. "You never head out on the trail without a few of the basics."

Oliver thought this over. "Too bad you don't have an umbrella in there," he said.

Dan snorted. "In this wind? You could kiss it good-bye in less than a minute. Or you could hang on to it and fly to Reno like Mary Poppins."

The rain was pelting down.

"You cold?" he asked Oliver.

Frank Oliver gave a small, sideways nod of agreement.

Dan thought about this. They were still scrunched into the hillside, sheltered only by the bushes. But it was far from ideal. It all depended on how long the rain lasted. Thunderstorms in the Sierra come and go, but they could last anywhere from a few minutes to a few hours… unless they were really serious. Then they could last all night.

The weather report had mentioned thunderstorms, but from the forecast, Dan hoped this would prove to be shorter, rather than longer.

Meanwhile, the rain bucketed down.

He reached into his pack and pulled out a plastic bag with some instant hand-warmers, and handed one to Oliver.

"Put your hands inside your jacket with one of these," he said. "Should help your hands, and maybe even warm up your core a little bit."

Oliver did as he was told.

"I'm hoping this won't go on too much longer," Dan said, to no response.

Dan considered using one of the hand warmers himself, but

decided to keep the rest for Oliver, if he needed them.

"If this guy only bought a few days of food, and he stays more or less following the PCT, then he should be at Ebbetts Pass in a couple of days," Dan said. "Do you have people watching that?"

Frank Oliver looked at him. The bar and the hand warmers seemed to have helped. "We have a bunch of people watching various places," he said.

Dan nodded. "But from here, he could go all sorts of directions. I mean, if he didn't follow the PCT, he could end up at about ten different trailheads."

Frank Oliver thought this over. Slowly he turned to Dan. "Look, we think we know who this guy is. And we think we know who he's working with. So we've got people watching them, too."

A thought occurred to Dan. "So you're tracking the guys you expect to meet up with him?"

Oliver nodded. "We have a lead on them. We think we know who they are. And we think we know where they are."

"And that is out this way?" Dan asked.

Oliver nodded. "Yeah. Last I heard."

"Where, exactly?" Dan asked.

Oliver thought this over again. He obviously didn't like to share too much information. Finally he said, "Wolf Creek."

He looked at Dan.

Dan chuckled. "Which one?"

Oliver looked at Dan in confusion.

"There's one just over that peak, and another one up here to the north," Dan explained.

Oliver still looked confused. "Is there one near Ebbetts Pass?" he asked.

Dan nodded. "Yeah, that's out here. Pretty straightforward,

right down this canyon. Then up and over the ridge."

Oliver stared out at the pouring rain.

"Do you think he's hiking in this shit?" Oliver asked.

"Not if he's got any brains," Dan said.

"Yeah, well, or maybe he is tough as nails," Oliver said.

"Or desperate," added Dan. "Really desperate."

The rain was sheeting down now. Dan looked again at Frank Oliver. The FBI agent was clearly miserable, with water dripping down his face. Dan thought he could still detect just a light but steady shiver in the man's body.

He decided to try conversation as a distraction. But it would require some effort. The noise of the rain reduced Dan to near shouting.

"Cal will be back at the trailhead," he said. "He'll stop anyone else from coming up here."

Oliver nodded.

"And the back-up team should be on its way," Dan continued.

"You think they'll try to hike in this weather?" Oliver asked, his voice cracking slightly with the strain.

Dan thought this over. "They're prepared for just about everything," he said, leaning into Oliver's ear. "But it all depends on how it looks where they are. If they see lightning near the pass, they may well wait for things to clear up a bit. No sense getting killed."

Oliver nodded.

chapter 29

At first Dan thought the noise was an animal nearby. A strange, scratchy sound seemed to come from somewhere behind his left shoulder.

Dan turned into the rain but couldn't see anything moving. Frankly, he couldn't see much at all, with the rain splashing into his face.

Then he heard the noise again, closer, and down by his hip.

He started, still thinking it was an animal.

And then he realized it was his radio, crackling into the storm.

Dan pulled it out and shouted into the radio, identifying himself.

When the radio crackled back, Dan couldn't hear much. He turned up the volume as high as possible.

"Dan, where are you?" It was Cindy in the dispatch office.

"Over St. Mary's Pass," Dan answered. "Down Clark's Fork Creek."

"Can you be more specific?" Cindy asked. "GPS coordinates?"

Dan pulled out his tracker and punched the buttons. It would take a few minutes for the device to find the satellites and give him a confirmed position.

Cindy was on the radio again. "Dan, are you okay? What are conditions like up there?"

Dan held his radio close to his mouth in answering. "Pretty

wild weather here," he said. "Just sheeting down rain, and we have lightning in the area, too."

Cindy asked him if he was safe.

"Reasonably safe," Dan answered. "We're well off the ridge, down in the canyon. Water is roaring by in the river. But we're okay."

His GPS came to life and gave Dan a reading.

He read the figures off to Cindy. "Does that help?" he asked.

"Okay," Cindy responded. "Just getting that plotted…"

Dan waited.

Cindy came back on the radio. "Dan, we've got a SPOT alert coming from that same area," she said. "Just a couple of miles down the canyon. Can you get there?"

Dan had already started to stand up. "Yes!" he yelled into the radio. "Give me the GPS for it!"

He handed his GPS to Frank Oliver so that the FBI agent could input the coordinates into the device.

While Cindy read off the numbers, Dan's mind was racing. The SPOT device wouldn't carry much information, just a request for emergency help. But there was no question in Dan's mind. The SPOT alert had come from the camp where Kristen was working.

And he was going to get there as quickly as possible.

Dan said as much to the radio.

Cindy told him that they had already scrambled a SAR chopper, but it would be a couple of hours before it got there. She also told him that a team was going to start in from Sonora Pass, but Dan was much closer.

Both she and Dan knew that if the weather didn't improve, the chopper wouldn't be able to get down into the canyon. The visibility was just too limited. And the other team was hours away.

Dan turned to Frank Oliver. "Let's go," he said.

It was clear who was in charge now. Dan started down the canyon, rain pouring over his jacket and face, his feet sloshing in the water wherever the trail was flat.

It was going to be an uncomfortable couple of miles.

chapter 30

The good news was that Oliver was trying hard to keep up with the brutal pace that Dan set. That, and the fact that the rain was beginning to ease up ever so slightly. Dan even noted an occasional lighter spot in the sky to the west. With some luck, the storm might be wrapping up.

But there was still water everywhere. On a normal hike, Dan would have tried to go around it, to find a path up above the trail and out of the trench that had captured the water. But not now. He was focused on only one thing: getting to Kristen and her clients as quickly as possible.

The sky was definitely lightening up now, and visibility was much better. Dan could see down the canyon, a mile or so, where a tributary stream joined the main flow of the Carson.

He pointed it out to Frank Oliver. "From the GPS coordinates, my guess is that they've camped somewhere near the mouth of that side canyon," he said, still hiking downhill as he talked.

After a few minutes, the FBI agent called out. "Are you just going to walk in there?" he asked. "I think we probably need a better plan than that."

Dan slowed his pace to allow Oliver to close the gap by a few yards. "I was thinking we would get close, and then creep on up…" Dan let the sentence trail off.

"This guy might have some pretty good intel," Oliver said. "If he is in contact with the rest of his gang, they may be able to let him know that there are people on the way."

That was not something that Dan had considered. He stared down the canyon as he hiked. He still couldn't see any sign of a tent or camp. He remembered that Kristen's tent was a pale blue. It would be hard to pick out against the granite boulders in the canyon.

"Got any ideas?" he asked.

"The basic rules are always the same," Oliver answered. "The high ground is an advantage. If we work our way up and to the left there, we might be able to see more, and at least get an idea of what the situation is."

Dan immediately noted a deer track leading in the direction that Oliver had suggested, and he took it without another word.

Now they were truly soaked. The game trail led them uphill through bushes that showered them with every step. Sometimes they had to push through thickets, and clamber over logs that would have been a minor inconvenience for the deer.

Dan heard a noise behind him and turned to see Oliver flat on his face in the mud, struggling to get up.

"You okay?" he asked.

"Great," said Oliver. He stood up and tried to wipe his hands on his pants to get some of the mud off. It didn't do much good. He looked up at Dan. "Let's go!"

Dan was now aiming for a small group of trees that would shield them from the lower canyon. The location would give them a good vantage point for their next step.

But as he got closer, he found the way blocked by a massive deadfall of large pine trees, lying in the brush of the canyon.

"Aw, shit!" he said.

Oliver came up behind him. "What the hell happened here?" he asked.

"It's probably from that big windstorm we had a few years ago," Dan answered. Some of the trees were two or three feet in diameter, and there were at least fifty trees down in front of them.

"This is going to be a real bushwhack," Dan said.

"Can we go around?" Oliver asked.

Dan looked up and down the slope. To go down would take them right into the open, close to the river. Above them, he could see more deadfalls.

"I think this is our best option," he said. "But be careful. These trees have been down for a while. Don't trust anything too much. And don't assume that these are all lying on the ground. There may be all kinds of crap underneath them, including big rocks or holes in the ground."

Frank Oliver nodded. "Okay. Let's do it."

Dan slowly climbed up and over the first log, then eased himself down into the manzanita and mountain misery on the far side.

He heard Oliver grunt and start climbing up onto the log.

This was not going to be any fun at all.

<h1 style="text-align:center">chapter 31</h1>

On the third log, Dan scratched his leg on the stump of a branch that he couldn't see as he lowered himself past it. That one would draw blood, he guessed.

A few trees later he heard Oliver swear behind him. "You okay?" He asked.

"Yeah, I just cracked my shin on a rock down here," Oliver replied.

At times Dan would try to use the top of a log as a lookout, to see down into the canyon, but he still couldn't even identify where the camp was, let alone any details.

A huge cluster of four logs had fallen down together, making a massive pile of trunks, branches and debris. Dan studied this as Frank Oliver caught up to him.

"That's a mess," Oliver said.

"No shit," Dan answered. "We can either go down through all those branches and probably rip our clothes to shreds…."

"You think we can get through there?" Oliver asked.

"Maybe," Dan said. "It ain't gonna be pretty. Or we can try to go up over these rocks and climb down the other side. Assuming we can climb down the other side." Neither option was appealing.

Frank Oliver looked up at the steep series of rocks that towered above them. "I think I can probably get up this," he said.

"Yeah," Dan replied. "But what if it looks like this on the other side? Can you get down it?"

While Oliver thought this over, Dan started to climb down through the branches of the trees, trying to keep out of the thickest snaggle of dead limbs.

As he felt his way down along one of the trunks, he saw a way to climb up on top of it. The tree was slick with the rain, but it was easier to walk along the top of the log than through the broken branches below.

He walked along the log, then found a way to hop across to another one. He could hear Oliver's heavy breathing behind him.

His log led to a dead end.

He turned around and climbed back uphill, hopping over to another log that led down into the brush. As he worked his way down the log, the slope got steeper and steeper.

Dan stopped and grabbed a branch that was sticking upright out of the log. The branch wobbled, but it gave Dan at least a little security.

Frank Oliver started to come down the log to stand next to Dan.

"This sucks," Dan said.

Oliver grabbed onto the wobbly branch with Dan. As the two men stood on the log, contemplating their next move, the branch suddenly snapped. Oliver slipped and began to fall. And as he fell, he reached out and caught Dan's leg.

The two of them fell down into the brush below.

Dan was surprised by how far they fell. The tree was only three feet in diameter, but it must have been hanging a good few feet off the ground, suspended by its branches and other trees below.

The two men crashed and slid down between the broken branches, Dan holding his hands over his face. He felt something crack underneath him, and then one of his feet hit the ground, and promptly slipped down the slope and sent him crashing down to land on his ass.

His GPS was gone. He knew that. He wondered if he had any broken bones. Adrenaline made that hard to tell. He wiggled his left foot. It seemed okay. His right leg was caught on something, and his foot was hanging up in the air above his head.

He looked around for Frank Oliver, but he couldn't see him.

A noise behind him, something between a grunt and a groan, told him that the FBI agent was at least alive.

Dan twisted and wiggled his right foot free, then wormed his way onto his stomach so that he could turn around.

Frank Oliver was behind Dan, but lower down the slope to the left. He appeared to have landed in a mass of manzanita which would have cushioned his fall, but a snapped branch could easily have speared him.

Just then Dan saw Oliver's head turn around and look at him.

"I've had better days," Oliver said.

Dan gave a short chuckle. "Did you break anything? Are you okay?" He could see the FBI agent moving different parts of his body, checking everything out.

"Not good," Oliver said. His poncho was draped around him like a shroud floating on the nearby branches.

Dan could see him struggling ineffectively on the mess of brush.

"My foot is fucked up," Oliver said.

Dan considered this. "Is it broken?" he asked. "Can you get out of there?"

Dan wriggled his body around on the rock that had stopped his fall. That hurt. Probably nothing broken, but there were some bad bruises there.

He worked his foot over toward Frank Oliver.

"Can you grab my foot and use it to pull yourself up?" Dan asked.

Oliver thought about this. "If I don't pull you down here…" he said.

"No, I'm good," Dan replied. He had a firm grip on a branch by his shoulder.

Oliver reached up and took hold of Dan's foot. As he pulled on Dan's leg, Dan could see Oliver's right foot struggling to get a purchase to help him up the slope. Oliver gave a gasp and stopped.

Dan waited.

"There's something really wrong with my left leg," Oliver said. "Somewhere below my knee." He was contorting himself to try and see down past his poncho.

"What do you want me to do?" Dan asked. "Can I get down there to help you?"

Oliver shook his head. "I don't think it will do any good," he said. "I'm fucked." He lay back in the dirt and bushes.

"Do you want me to see if I can get you out of there?" Dan asked.

Oliver shook his head again. "Nope. But I would like to get somewhere to sit more comfortably."

Dan clambered down and placed both hands under Oliver's arms. He began to pull while Oliver struggled to push with his one good leg.

After wrestling himself into position for a few minutes, Oliver precariously perched himself on a rock in the midst of the fallen trees. He looked at Dan.

"Good enough," he said. "Now I think you should get down to

that camp and see what's going on. I'll be okay here."

Dan thought this over. "Yeah, but if I run into trouble down there, you end up stuck up here for a long time."

Oliver reached down into the bushes and came up with Dan's GPS unit.

"Call it in on your radio," Oliver suggested. "Tell them I'm here. They'll get here eventually. Meanwhile, you need to get a move on."

"Why don't I just leave the radio with you?" Dan asked.

"Because if you need it down there, you won't have it," Oliver replied. "Go ahead."

"So I am just supposed to leave you here?" Dan asked.

"Look, my leg is fucked up," Oliver said. "I am in pain, but it's manageable. If you pull me out of here, then what? I won't be able to walk. I can't put weight on my foot."

"I could help you," Dan said.

"So that would make two ineffective people instead of one effective person. Go on. Get moving. I'll be fine. When the SAR team gets here, they can deal with this better than you, anyway."

Dan realized the FBI agent was probably right. He called in their position and Frank Oliver's condition, then looked up out of the brush to the clearing sky.

He took a deep breath and slowly started moving.

chapter 32

Dan painstakingly climbed out of the brush and up over rocks and branches. The smell of pine and juniper flooded his nostrils. From the top of the next log, Dan saw a game trail on the ground below that led through the trees for a good fifty feet.

Then another logjam blocked this path. This time Dan stayed to the left, trying to keep out of the branches, and closer to the main trunks of the trees. That worked, and Dan eventually eased out onto a large log, only to find that it was the last one. Beyond the log he could see only brush, and, miraculously, the grove of trees.

He looked back and realized that he couldn't even see where Frank Oliver was lying. He was on his own.

From the small grove of trees, Dan could now see well down into the canyon. With his eyes he followed the river down and spotted a yellow tent near a clump of trees perched on the edge of the river.

Between the trees he began to make out more tents, but he didn't see any people.

He waited for a few minutes, but still didn't see any movement by the tents. The river was absolutely roaring below them, crashing along with all the rain that had fallen.

Dan slowly crept down the hill, aiming for a large log that lay some fifty yards closer to the camp.

He slipped out below the trees and into the brush that covered the hillside above the camp, picking his way as quietly as possible. He was now close enough to count at least four tents. One of them, a pale blue one farthest from the river, looked like Kristen's.

He crept downhill, still lugging Cal's shotgun, and dropped in behind the log. He sat down to catch his breath and leaned his back against the log.

The log had fallen downhill, its top end towards the river. Dan thought that the few rotting branches there might give him more cover, and he sidled along behind the log to get down there.

He peered out between the branches, and was startled to see Kristen walking toward him, only twenty feet away. Before he could say anything, she saw him as well, and stopped dead with a jerk.

After doing a second take, she stared at him, and then started walking over to the log.

"What the hell are you doing here?" she asked. She did not look happy.

Dan held his finger up in front of his lips, then waved her over to him. When she was just the other side of the log, he began to speak.

"Is everyone okay here?" he asked in a quiet voice.

"Why are you whispering?" Kristen asked him, now clearly annoyed. "Everything's fine. We had a little storm. Nothing major. Lots of noise."

Dan held his hand up in apology. "We got a SPOT alert from around here." he said, still speaking in a soft undertone. "We're chasing a fugitive, potentially dangerous, down this canyon. And we got a SPOT alert. So I want to make sure. Is everyone okay?"

Kristen slowly walked around the end of the dead tree to join Dan. The two of them looked at the camp. No movement came from any of the tents.

"What kind of fugitive?" she asked skeptically.

"We're not sure," Dan admitted. "But it could be one of the people who killed that guy in the mine over by Big Hill Road."

Kristen thought this over. "I didn't hear anything during the storm. But I couldn't have in the storm." She shook her head. "It was deafening. Do you think he's around here?"

Dan nodded. "We think he headed down this canyon towards Wolf Creek. And we were only an hour or two behind him."

Kristen glanced around nervously. "And he's around here?"

"He could be," Dan agreed.

Kristen continued to look around her. "Who is 'we'?"

Dan pointed with his chin. "An FBI agent is up there, hurt," he said. "Cal is at the trailhead. There's a SAR team on the way."

The zipper on one of the tents opened up. Dan and Kristen ducked down behind the branches to watch.

"That's Ian," Kristen whispered. "Undergrad, grew up somewhere back east."

They watched as Ian walked over to one of the tables set up under a rain tarp. He looked around nervously, then took something from his pocket and put it on the table. Dan guessed it was the SPOT unit.

Dan could see motion in one of the other tents now. "How many people are here?" he asked Kristen.

"Five plus me," she said. "Two in that tent, a couple, then three more singles over behind the tables. And I'm over there." She pointed with her chin.

A woman climbed out of one of the tents and greeted Ian. "Everybody okay?" they heard her call out.

Voices called back to her. Dan looked at Kristen.

"Maybe he never made it this far," she said. "Or maybe he went past us during the storm."

"Yeah," Dan agreed. "Unless he's hanging around here." And he peered up the sides of the canyon. All they could hear was the roaring of the river.

chapter 33

By the time the SAR team arrived, Dan had checked out the area around the camp, and found no sign of anyone else.

"The rain would have washed away any tracks anyway," one of the SAR team said.

They were in the process of putting Frank Oliver on a stretcher.

Dan looked at Frank Oliver. The FBI agent was clearly thinking the situation over.

"If he's around here now, he won't want to be seen," Oliver said. "And it won't be hard for him to stay hidden. But I'd still want to make sure that everyone here is aware of the danger."

Dan looked over at the team of scientists. "I'm not sure they are going to want to leave," he said.

Oliver looked at him. "Until we find this guy, or make sure he isn't around here, they need to get out," Oliver said.

Dan suddenly realized that he could hear a helicopter. He looked at the SAR leader. "Are they flying him out of here?" he asked.

The chopper came sailing down the middle of the canyon. "It looks like it," one of the rescue team said. "The chopper was already on its way, and it will make this a lot easier."

For the next thirty minutes the helicopter created chaos at the camp. The rain tarps were blown away, tents shuddered, and people were yelling and running to grab things and hold them down.

Meanwhile, the SAR team loaded Frank Oliver into the chopper and watched him fly away into the twilight.

After the chopper left, Kristen came over with a slightly pudgy fortyish man who looked like he was trying to grow a beard without much success. He wore blue jeans, and the pocket of his shirt was stained where a pen had leaked.

"Dan, this is Dr. Hollister, from Nevada Reno," Kristen said. "This is his project."

It wasn't an easy conversation. Dan knew that the smart and safe thing to do was to hike everyone out of the canyon tonight with the SAR team. But he also understood why Dr. Hollister would not want to leave.

It helped that one of the SAR team members was a deputy in the Sheriff's Department. His name tag read Gilmore. Dan didn't know him well, but the two of them were able to convince Hollister that his team might well be in danger in the camp.

"So I'm supposed to leave all this stuff here?" Hollister asked. "There's some expensive equipment that I can't afford to lose."

Dan looked over the camp. The sun had already set. The light wouldn't last much longer.

He turned to Deputy Gilmore. "Are you carrying?" he asked.

The Deputy nodded.

"Want to stay here tonight?" Dan asked. "The two of us could watch things. And they're already planning to send in a big group tomorrow to search the whole area."

He turned to Dr. Hollister. "That's assuming that we could use your gear for the night," he said. "We'd need a tent and a couple of sleeping bags."

"You're welcome to my bag and tent," the young guy Kristen

had identified as Ian offered.

Dan thanked him. "Why don't you show me?" he said.

The SAR team was now packed up and ready to leave.

Dan walked over to Ian's tent with him. After the student had shown Dan his gear, Dan grabbed him briefly by the elbow. "Was that you that sent the SPOT alert?" he asked.

Ian swallowed guiltily and took his time before answering. "Yeah. Sorry. That storm freaked me out."

"And that's why you put the SPOT transmitter on the table when you got up, right?" Dan asked.

Ian nodded, staring down at his boots.

"Two things," Dan said, holding up two fingers. "One: always check with your team leader before activating that thing. You're not the best person to decide what is an emergency. That's why Dr. Hollister is in charge." He paused.

Ian nodded again.

"And two: Because of that SPOT, we got a chopper here tonight," Dan continued. "And that got our FBI agent to a hospital now, rather than having him get carried out by these guys." He waved at the SAR team. "Or wait until morning. I don't think anyone is going to complain about that."

Kristen walked over to Dan and led him to the table under the tarp. She showed him the stove and the cache of bear cans, each one labeled for breakfast, lunch, or dinner.

Dan caught Greg Gilmore's eye. "Looks like we have all we need for food."

Gilmore agreed. "I'll take Dr. Hollister's tent, if that's okay."

"Fine," Dan agreed.

They watched the SAR team hiking slowly back up into the shadows of the canyon.

"I guess we take turns on watch," the deputy said.

"Yeah, that should be fun," Dan replied dryly.

"Do you want to cook?" Gilmore asked, pointing to the bear cans. "Or do you want me to do it? I'm pretty good at boiling water."

Dan watched as Gilmore walked over to one of the cans marked Dinner and opened it up. "Looks like we have lots of choices," he said.

But Dan wasn't paying attention. He was looking up into the trees above the canyon.

"You go ahead and get some dinner," he said. "I think I'm going to take a look around."

Gilmore looked at him. "You really think that perp is hanging around here?" he asked.

"I don't know," Dan admitted. "But I sure as hell don't want to find out the hard way."

chapter 34

It was a long, cold night. But it was also a quiet night.

"No sign of anybody," Gilmore said to Dan when he woke him up the next morning. "I think that guy is somewhere to hell and gone."

Dan's radio had already crackled to life this morning, and it sounded as if their canyon was about to be invaded by a major expeditionary force.

The first to arrive was another chopper. But this one didn't land. It just flew up and down the canyon, searching with both visual and infrared.

An hour or so later a group came in on horseback, including two tracking dogs.

Dan was pleased to see that one of the men on horseback was Cal.

"See anything last night?" he asked Dan.

Dan shook his head.

Cal reached into his pack and pulled out a small paper bag. He tossed it to Dan. "Maggie sent you a muffin."

Dan laughed. "Thanks!" he said. "Much better than instant oatmeal."

"I figured," Cal said. He looked at two men who were working with the dogs. "I don't know what they think they are going to do."

"After that storm?" Dan said. "Not much."

"Still," Cal said, "if this guy is armed…"

"And we have more people on the way?" Dan asked.

"Oh hell, we've got the whole Seventh Fleet in here," Cal said. "There are LEOs at every trailhead: Ebbetts Pass, Highland Lakes, Sonora Pass, down at Clark's Fork…"

"And Wolf Creek?" Dan asked.

Cal nodded. "Yeah, watching that. That might be where he's headed. So that one's undercover."

Dan gave him a questioning look.

Cal shrugged. "They're hoping to catch his friends, too," he said. "There's a lot of ground to cover here."

Dan agreed. "Bad enough when somebody is trying to be found. This guy is trying to stay lost."

"We're putting huge resources out here, but…" Cal replied.

Dan watched as the dog teams started moving down the canyon.

Cal looked at Dan. "You look like hell, Dan," he said.

Dan laughed. "Thanks. We took turns keeping watch last night."

"I figured," Cal said. "Did Gary keep you entertained with his hunting stories?"

Dan shook his head. "Nope. He slept and I watched. Then I slept and he watched. We didn't spend a whole lot of time in conversation."

"Consider yourself lucky," Cal noted. "He's been known to go on for hours."

Dan's radio crackled again. It was Steve Matson, telling Dan that he could take the rest of the day off if he wanted.

Dan told him he'd think about it. Which he did, for less than a minute.

Cal had overheard the conversation. "If you leave now, you might miss out on the big reward," he said.

"What's that?" Dan asked.

"There's a hundred-thousand-dollar reward for this guy Willyers' phone," Cal explained. "I guess his company really wants to find that phone."

Dan could see that the men with the dogs were already heading back into camp.

"That didn't last long," he said to Cal.

Cal called out to them. "Did you forget your poop bags?" he asked.

The men didn't answer until they were much closer.

"There's a stream down there about a hundred and fifty yards down," one of the men said. "And it's totally blown out. No possible way to get past that."

"That's from the storm," Dan said.

All three men nodded.

"And if he didn't get across that yesterday afternoon…" Cal said.

"Then he's still on this side of the creek," Dan finished for him.

chapter 35

But he wasn't on their side of the creek. The massive search team spent days scouring the area and found no sign of the mysterious fugitive.

They had closed down the Pacific Crest Trail for four days as they roamed across the Sierra. The Marines had joined the search on the second day, working their way up from the Mountain Warfare base on the east side.

The Naval Air Station over at Lemoore sent choppers over every day, complete with infrared cameras to search. Search parties entered the Sierra from six different trailheads with search dogs.

They had placed flyers at all the trailheads and debriefed every hiker they met on the trail. They had requested help from the public, from anyone who might have been hiking in the area.

And there was no sign of the missing hiker.

Dan was at the Summit Ranger Office a few days later when he got a call from Frank Oliver.

"I just wanted to thank you for the help up there in the mountains," Oliver said.

"I didn't help you much," Dan demurred. "I left you on the side of the canyon with a broken ankle. But you're welcome."

"Turns out it was a spiral fracture of the fibula," Oliver said.

"Broken leg," Dan said. "Even better,"

"Well, anyway, we didn't catch this guy, haven't caught him yet," Oliver said. "But you did a helluva job. So thanks."

"Do we know any more about who he is?" Dan asked.

"We have a pretty good idea," Oliver said. "There was a group of nasty Russians in an SUV over by Wolf Creek. We'd been tracking them for some time."

"And they were waiting for this guy?" Dan asked.

"We think so," Oliver agreed. "But from what we can tell, those guys are as confused as we are. He never showed up, and they don't seem to have any idea why not. Or where he is."

"Do you think he could still be up there somewhere?" Dan asked.

"It's possible. At this point anything is possible," Oliver said. "But from what we can see, he's gone silent. He may have decided to double-cross his friends, or just bail out of their operation."

Dan could sense the frustration in Oliver's voice.

"Well, if his friends are also confused, at least we were looking in the right places," Dan said.

Frank Oliver snorted. "Or maybe at least looking for the right guy? Right now, we don't even know that."

Dan considered this. "But what about the phone?" he asked. "Didn't Travis' story line up with Willyer's cell phone pings?"

"Yeah," Oliver admitted. "If it really was the guy with Travis. Could have been anyone in Bridgeport at the same time…"

"Did you ever get another ping from that phone?" Dan asked.

Oliver hesitated. "Maybe," he said. "If we did, it was a day later, and it wasn't for long."

"And where did that signal come from?" Dan asked.

"Hard to tell," Oliver said. "But maybe somewhere between Sonora and Bridgeport. It's not very accurate, you know."

"Uh huh," Dan grunted. "But that would also be in that same area…"

"Maybe," Oliver said. "Maybe it was."

"Do you know who he called?" Dan asked.

"He didn't call, he texted," Oliver said. "To a burner phone bought for cash in Las Vegas a couple of weeks ago. Not much to go on there."

Dan had to agree. There was not much to go on.

"So what happens now?" Dan asked. "Are you still working on this? Or what?"

"Officially, I'm on medical leave," Oliver replied. "I'll put in a few days in the office, but they've offered me six weeks and I'm going to take it."

"Sounds good," Dan said.

"Listen," Oliver said. "If you hear anything from some hikers or anything, I know you'll report it. But I'd appreciate it if you'd let me know directly, too."

"Okay." Dan didn't like that much, but he understood why Oliver was asking.

"Any chance you might be going up that way any time in the future?" Oliver asked.

"I guess you know that they've pretty much wrapped up the search now," Dan said. "They never did find anything…"

"I know," Oliver said. "I can't believe we missed the guy by that much. Or that little."

It seemed to Dan that Oliver still had something on his mind.

"And you still think the guy we were following was the right guy?" Dan asked.

"Officially, he's a person of interest," Oliver said. "But if I had to bet, I'd bet he's absolutely the guy we're looking for. And his friends are looking for him. And I wonder if he didn't just hole up somewhere up there and is waiting for all this to blow over."

Dan considered this. "If he had a day to hike from that camp, he could be in a lot of places," Dan said. "And he could go quite a few days on minimal food. He could be almost anywhere."

"Exactly," Oliver said. "So just keep your eyes open…"

"Mine, and everyone else's," Dan said. "We have signs and notices about him at every trailhead in the northern Sierra."

chapter 36

Later that day, Dan was delighted to see Kristen and Dr. Hollister walk into the ranger station.

After exchanging greetings, Dr. Hollister got right to the point. "I'm assuming that we are now cleared to go back in and finish our research?" he asked.

Dan made a quick call to Steve Matson. Matson wasn't very happy with the idea and wanted to check with the FBI and the Sheriff's Department.

Dan passed on the news to Dr. Hollister.

"So when exactly are you going to reopen the area?" Hollister asked.

Dan could see a faint white area around the scientist's mouth.

"When we do, you guys get first priority," he said.

Kristen gave a sigh. "They just want to get back to work, Dan," she said. "Me, too."

Dan nodded. "I should know something more by the end of the day."

"Hey," Kristen said suddenly. "Would it make a difference if you came along with us? Could you do that?" She sounded hopeful in a way that Dan found very attractive.

Dan sadly shook his head. "I doubt it. If the area is closed because it's dangerous, they won't want anyone in there. And I don't know if I can get the time, anyway. We're routing all the PCT hikers through Highland Lakes now."

"They've announced that the search is over," Hollister said. "They've all packed out of there. So how long until someone decides that it's safe?"

Dan agreed. "Yep. But it's not my call. That one has to come from law enforcement."

"Would it make a difference if you joined us?" Hollister asked again, looking at Kristen. "Because if that's all it takes, we'd be happy to have you join us. We just want to finish our work and get our stuff out of there."

The idea of making the trip with Kristen got Dan's attention. Maybe there was a way he could convince his boss.

"Let me see what I can do," he said. And Kristen smiled at him. Dan turned around and walked into his office, realizing that he might just be blushing a little. And furious about that.

Once in his office, he started to pick up his phone, only to have Doris knock on his door.

"Cal Healey is on line two," she said.

Dan picked up the phone.

"Hi, Cal," he said.

"I understand that you want to escort your grlfriend into the West Carson," Cal began.

"What?" Dan was confused. "No, they just want to get in there to get their equipment. That's way out of my league to make that decision."

"Uh huh," Cal said. "That's not what I heard." He was clearly enjoying the conversation. "But listen, I think we're going to decide that it's okay for them to go in there for two days. One day in, and one day out. Just enough time to pack up their gear and get back out of there."

"Okay," Dan said guardedly. "I'm not sure they'll be happy with that."

"Yeah, well, the other option is that they don't go at all," Cal continued. "And my boss has decided that we need to accompany them and make sure that the area is safe."

"So how many of your guys will go?" Dan asked.

"Oh, no, no, no," Cal muttered. "It's not how many of our guys. It's me. And somebody from the Forest Service. Do you know anybody in the Forest Service?"

Dan chuckled. "Seriously? You and me? We're the escort?"

Cal snorted. "You're the escort, Dan. Not me. I'm married. My guess is that Matson is already on the other line, waiting to tell you all about this."

Dan glanced at his office phone. The other line was blinking.

"So when do we leave?" he asked Cal.

"See you in the morning, Sunshine," Cal said. "Don't expect another muffin."

Dan went back into the back office to take the call from Steve Matson.

"I have good news and bad news," Steve began.

At home that night, Dan noticed the blinking red light that told him he had a message on his answering machine. He punched the button to hear the voice of Bruce Spielman.

"Hey, buddy, Bruce here. Hope you are doing okay. Give me a call when you get a chance. I've got more news for you."

The voice in the message sounded subdued compared to Bruce's usual bluster.

Dan dialed Bruce's number and waited, this time for four rings, before Bruce answered his call.

"Hi, Dan," he said quietly.

"How are you doing, Bruce?" Dan asked him. "How's the mining?"

"Not good," Bruce admitted. "I haven't been down there again."

"Well, there's always next week," Dan said.

"Yeah," Bruce agreed. "I think I'm going to have to hold off for a bit."

He waited for Dan to ask why. Dan finally gave in. "How come?"

"I've got kind of a health issue right now," Bruce said. "Poison oak."

"Ohhh…" From his childhood, Dan knew how bad this could

be. "I'm sorry, Bruce."

"It's my own damn fault," Bruce said. "It's that bushwhack down into the canyon. There's just too much of the stuff to avoid. I did okay on the way down, but on the way back up, it was much worse, much harder."

"Did you go to the doctor?" Dan asked.

"Oh yeah," Bruce said. "I'm covered in the stuff. They gave me a couple of injections and some pills to take and some stuff to put on it."

"Wow," Dan sympathized. "You've really got it bad."

"You know how bad it is?" Bruce asked. "When I took my shirt off, the doctor burst out laughing and said it was the worst case he'd ever seen."

Dan chuckled. "It doesn't sound like your doctor has much of a bedside manner."

"Well, he told me I wouldn't die from it, but I'd be uncomfortable as hell for a while."

"Sorry to hear it," Dan said. "I guess this slows down the income from mining operations for a while, huh?"

"For a while, anyway," Bruce said.

"How long does the doctor think it will take for it to clear up?" Dan asked.

"A couple or few weeks," Bruce said. "It all depends on a lot of different factors. That's what the doc says."

Dan thought about Bruce's mining plans. "You know, it's not going to get any easier to get down there," he said. "That poison oak is tough stuff, and there's really no easy way to get rid of it."

"Yeah, I know," Bruce said. "I've gotta make this work Dan. I know there's gold down there."

"Well," Dan said. "If you want my advice…" he left the

sentence hanging.

"Sure," Bruce answered. "That's what I'm paying for, right?"

"And worth every penny you are paying," Dan said. "I'd look for an easier way to make a buck. One that doesn't involve bushwhacking through poison oak."

"Yeah," Bruce agreed. "I think next time instead of going straight into the canyon over the ridge, I am going to work my way up the river from down below… maybe that will be easier."

Dan blew air out between his lips. "That's a long slog," he said. "And that river runs from side to side in the canyon. You'll get cliffed out on every turn, and have to cross the river to keep going."

"Yeah, I know," Bruce said. "But I think it's worth a try."

"And the water will only be low enough for that at the end of the summer," Dan reminded him. "And there will still be poison oak, too."

"You got that right," Bruce said. "I learned that the hard way."

Dan smiled. "Well, I hope you feel better," he said.

"Thanks, Dan," Bruce said. "If that lower river route doesn't work, I might try coming down river from above, like up by Lyons Dam."

Dan's eyebrows shot up. "Good luck with that," he said. He was glad his own trip promised to be a lot less challenging.

chapter 38

The next morning Dan arrived at the Sonora Pass trailhead to find it full of vehicles. There were still the trail angels for the PCT hikers, armed with information and maps on how to head north without taking the PCT.

And then there were the horse trailers clogging the parking lot. A van with the University of Nevada Reno logo on the side was parked there as well. And Cal's SUV.

After a quick look around, he found Kristen over by the packers, discussing how she thought their camp might fit onto the four pack mules that were tethered in the trees.

Dan arrived in time to hear her tell Randy Fuller that it had taken six mules to pack them in.

"Well, you've got four mules today, because that's all I could get," Dan heard the man say. "So let's hope we can fit this all on four mules. At least the food's all gone, right?"

"That's what I've been saying," Kristen said. "We haven't been there for a week. The food is still there."

The packer did not look optimistic.

Dan looked at the mules again. He counted six. "Aren't there five pack mules, plus the one you're riding?" he asked.

Randy Fuller looked up to see Dan, and shook his hand.

"Nope, that other mule is for the Sheriff to ride." he said.

Just then Cal emerged from the outhouse. He saw Dan and walked over.

"You're riding today?" Dan asked.

"Hell yes, I'm riding," Cal said. "With my knee it would take me two days to hike in there. And you'd probably have to chopper me back out."

Dan looked around. "Who else is going?" he asked, of no one in particular. He looked at Kristen.

"Bryan and I are hiking in," she said. "And two of the students are supposed to join us. But they're not here yet."

"Do we wait for them?" Dan asked. He noticed that Kristen was on a first name basis with Dr. Hollister. He knew that was normal, just a part of good customer service on her end. It still niggled at him.

Dan grabbed his pack out of his SUV and strapped it on. "No need to wait for the mules," he said. "We might as well get going. Your students can follow us in when they get here." He said this last to Dr. Hollister.

"We'll be here for at least another hour," the packer said. "We can let them know."

"And if we leave, we'll leave word with our angel friends here," Cal said.

Dan walked over to the trail and offered Hollister the opportunity to go first.

"No, no," Hollister said. "You are both going to hike faster than me. You go ahead."

Dan looked at Kristen. She motioned him to go first.

"Let me know if I'm going too fast for you," he said, and then started hiking up the trail toward Sonora Peak.

The trail climbed steeply at first, straight up from the highway, and Dan loved the feeling of working hard, easing into a steady pace and rocking it up the mountain.

Behind him, he could occasionally hear the light tread of Kristen as she followed him up.

A mile into the hike, Dan paused at the first big switchback. He looked back to see Kristen only a few feet behind him. That surprised him. Dr. Hollister was not in view.

"Did we lose your professor?" he asked Kristen.

"He probably stopped to look at something," Kristen said. Dan was even more surprised to note that Kristen didn't seem to be breathing any harder than Dan was.

"You're in pretty good shape," he said to her. "It's nice to hike with someone who has the same pace."

Kristen smiled wryly at him. "I was trying not to slow you down."

Dan laughed out loud. "I don't think that's a problem."

He grinned at her. "Should we wait for Bryan?"

Kristen shook her head. "He knows where he's going. And he likes to hike at his own pace," she said. "Let's keep going."

Dan turned and started up the mountain again. He felt great. It was a perfect morning in the Sierra. At ten thousand feet the sky was a breathtakingly deep blue and contrasted against the almost black volcanic rock of Sonoma Peak. A few mule ears were just beginning to bloom.

From behind him, he heard Kristen ask; "Why aren't you married, Dan?"

That came out of nowhere. He gave a short, harsh chuckle. "I was once," he told her, letting his voice carry over his shoulder. "It didn't work out."

"Oh, I'm sorry," Kristen answered.

Dan shook his head. "No, it's a fair question. We met in college. A few years later, she decided it wasn't working for her." He still felt a tug in his gut when he talked about it.

"How about you?" he asked.

"No. Never," she said.

He stopped to turn and look at her. "You must have had a few offers," he suggested, and immediately regretted it. What if she hadn't? But she must have had offers.

She shook her head. "It was never right," was all she said.

She smiled up at him, above her on the trail, and he turned around and started hiking again. The trail soon had his attention, making him work up the hill, and repaying him with new views at each turn and rise.

That didn't keep him from thinking about what she had asked, and why she had asked it. It seemed to him that most of the reasons were good. That took away the tug in his gut, and lifted him up as he hiked the trail. That was good, he decided.

And Kristen seemed to be humming quietly behind him, clearly enjoying herself. That was good, too.

"Yep," Dan thought. "It's a perfect morning in the Sierra."

He continued to think that as he and Kristen contoured around Sonora Peak, passed above Wolf Creek Lake, and then crossed over the pass into the canyon of the East Fork of the Carson River.

They stopped at the pass to take in the view.

"It looks pretty different from the last time I was here," Dan said.

Kristen leaned into him as he pointed out the route that he and Frank Oliver had taken around the far side of Sonoma Peak. He could smell her. Was it perfume? Shampoo? Something nice, he thought.

As he turned back towards her, he saw motion on the mountain behind them.

"The pack train is catching up to us," he said.

Kristen turned to see.

"Let's see how far we can get before they catch us," she said. And struck off down the trail with long strides.

Dan was happy to follow her downhill.

<h1 style="text-align:center">chapter 39</h1>

They very nearly made it all the way to camp. The mules passed them just below the mass of fallen trees that had led to Frank Oliver's broken ankle.

As the mules rode by, Cal slowed and handed Dan some folded papers.

"Your pal at the FBI wanted me to give these to you," he said. "Pretty interesting. Check out the dates."

With the mules now heading down the canyon toward the camp, Dan unfolded what turned out to be some aerial photos. Kristen leaned to look over his shoulder.

After staring at the photos for a few minutes, Kristen said, "That's this canyon." She pointed with her finger. "And that's about where our camp is."

Dan looked at the other photo. "These are the same place," he said.

Kristen pointed to a lighter-colored smear on one of the maps. "But what's that?"

Dan remembered what Cal had said. He checked the date and time of each photo. He held up the first photo. "This one is from two weeks ago."

Kristen was reading the info on the other map. "This one was yesterday," she said. "That big smear is new."

Dan looked again. It looked like a section of the mountain had exploded. Or eroded.

He nodded. "That storm must have caused a major slide up here," he said. "It looks like a huge gash in the mountain."

"Where did he get these?" Kristen asked.

Dan smiled. "Google. Or a surveillance satellite. Who knows…?"

"Pretty cool," Kristen said. "We should go check that out."

"In our free time?" Dan asked.

But Kristen was already walking down the trail towards the camp.

By the time they arrived in camp, the packer had already taken down the main rain tarp and was picking through the rest of the gear to see what would fit where.

Dan quickly pulled his own tent out of his pack and set it up, not too far from Kristen's. She was busy identifying the bear canisters that they would need for tonight and tomorrow morning. The rest got stacked in a pile for the packer.

Cal made a motion to catch Dan's eye.

"Did you check out those photos?" he asked.

"That's an impressive slide there," Dan said.

"I just wonder what else the FBI has photos of," Cal said. "Makes you think about your own backyard, doesn't it?"

Dan grinned. "Don't you get those from the DEA?" he asked Cal.

"I don't," Cal said. "Somebody might, but I don't. I think they stop a lot higher up than me."

While they were talking, Dan noticed that Cal was scanning the sides of the canyon.

"Are you still looking for our friend?" he asked Cal.

Cal shrugged, but didn't take his eyes off the slopes. "I just hope he's not looking for us," he said to Dan.

Dan shook his head. "What the hell happened?" he asked Cal. "I mean, we followed that guy. We were only an hour or two behind him."

"You stopped hiking in the storm," Cal said. "Maybe he didn't. That would give him another couple of hours on you."

"Yeah," Dan agreed. "But a couple of hours in a total downpour. He can't have made very good speed in that."

Cal kept staring at the slopes. "Or maybe he just found a place to hole up and he's waiting for things to calm down."

"And then what? Then he hikes out like nothing ever happened?" Dan asked.

Cal shrugged again. "I don't know," he said. "But from what I got from your FBI friends, I'd believe just about anything. He could be anywhere."

Dan followed Cal's gaze towards the steep hillsides above them. The hair on the back of his neck stood up as he thought about it.

chapter 40

"What do you think the story is, here?" Dan asked Cal.

Cal shrugged. "Officially? We don't know. Officially we're pursuing a number of leads in the investigation."

Dan nodded. "Yeah, I know. But we know that Theo Willyers is dead. Right?"

"Oh, yeah," Cal agreed. "And not a pretty death, either."

"Right. And we know that somebody got his cell phone and his ID…" Dan continued.

"Looks like it," Cal said. "That's why the feds and everybody else suddenly started jumping on this."

"And this guy that Travis met," Dan suggested. "Who the hell is he?"

Cal nodded. "That's one question, all right. Who is he?" Cal paused and looked around at the slopes above them. "And where is he?"

Dan sighed in frustration.

"You want to know what I think?" Cal asked. Then he continued, without waiting for an answer. "I think this guy up here is part of some kind of gang that kidnapped that Willyers guy."

"Yeah," Dan encouraged him to continue.

Cal shrugged. "Somehow they got him off the PCT," Cal continued. "Pulled him off, drugged him, offered him a ride. Who knows?"

Dan nodded, but kept silent.

"And once they got him, they beat the living hell out of him," Cal continued. "They beat the sonofabitch until he spilled his guts and told them how to access his accounts."

Dan winced. "You'd think there would be some kind of system in place…"

"You'd think," Cal said. "But don't forget that this Willyers guy or whatever his name was, he was the smartest damn bunny in the hutch. Facial recognition and all that."

"And it was the whole point of his company," Dan added.

"Right, he was living proof that the whole thing worked." Cal said. And then he corrected himself, "He was living proof."

"But what about the other guys?" Dan asked. "Didn't you tell me that there was an SUV full of bad guys where they found his body?"

Cal nodded. "Oh yeah, he had help. We just don't know who they were."

"But didn't you say that they were waiting for this guy at Wolf Creek?"

Cal looked at him. "Did I say that?"

Dan nodded. "I think so."

"I can't remember if I said that," Cal replied. "And I can't remember if they told me that, or if I was allowed to tell you that."

Dan chuckled at him. "You need to get your story straight, Cal," he said.

Cal smiled. "It sure isn't my story," he said. "I'm just sitting on the outside, trying to figure out what's going on. And the guys on the inside aren't sharing much info."

"You mean the FBI?" Dan asked.

"Maybe," Cal nodded. "Somebody with the feds is managing this whole thing. And they aren't telling me their innermost secrets."

"Why don't they just arrest the guys that were waiting at Wolf Creek?" Dan asked.

Cal sighed. "It ain't that simple, Ranger Dan."

"Okay, I give up," Dan said. "Why isn't it that simple?"

Cal sighed again. "When you arrest somebody, you tell everybody he knows that you are onto him. And some of the people he knows are probably more important, and may not know that we know about them."

"Do we know about them?" Dan asked.

Cal laughed. "How the hell should I know? I'm not getting their memos, remember?"

Dan nodded.

"But what I do know is that they haven't arrested anyone, which tells me they are still watching people and maybe hoping to get more information. And maybe find out more about who's behind this whole thing."

"As far as you know," Dan reminded him.

Cal laughed out loud. "Yeah, as far as I know." He looked at Dan. "And God knows I don't know much."

"I've always said that about you," Dan said with a grin.

"And in this case, you are sure as hell correct," Cal agreed.

chapter 41

Dan heard voices in the camp and turned to see that Bryan Hollister and two young men had joined them. They immediately began to organize the camp and get their gear together for the hike out the next day.

Cal looked at Dan. "Do you want to take a walk?" he asked. "I don't think there's anything for us to do around here right now."

Dan followed Cal out of camp, heading further down into the canyon.

"You think it's okay to leave them there?" he asked Cal.

"You've got five people there," Cal said. "And we're not looking for a serial killer. There'd be no point in him attacking them. Hell, if he's in the area and wanted the food, he would have taken it by now."

"So where are you going?" Dan asked, as he followed Cal's limping gate down the canyon.

Cal stopped and turned around to look at Dan. "Both you and I think the guy was headed down this way, because he was trying to get to his pals down on Wolf Creek."

"Assuming that they were his pals," Dan said.

"Right," Cal agreed.

"And assuming the FBI is right about which Wolf Creek," Dan said.

"Yeah," Cal agreed again. "But at least his pals were waiting for him there, not over at this one." His chin pointed over the ridge toward Wolf Creek Lake.

"Okay, so let's say he's hiking down here," Dan prompted Cal.

"Right," Cal said. "It's a fucking apocalyptic downpour. He can't cross the river, because it's blowing pure white water."

Dan looked at the East Fork of the Carson, which was now eased back into a reasonable shape.

"And up ahead, he is going to run into that side canyon, which was roaring as well," Cal continued. "So what would you do?"

"Go back over St. Mary's Pass?" Dan suggested.

"I was waiting there, remember?" Cal asked. "But yeah, maybe he bailed out over Boulder Lake or something. But we had people at all those trailheads. I don't think he hiked out there. So the probability is that he didn't do that."

"Which would leave him around here, somewhere," Dan said.

"Which would leave him somewhere," Cal agreed. "Somewhere around here."

The two men continued walking down the canyon, parallel to the river. Within a few minutes they had reached the creek that came down from the west side of the canyon into the Carson.

"When the guys with the dogs showed up, they said that this was impassable," Dan said to Cal.

The creek had fallen in the days since the storm. Dan saw at least three places where he thought he could cross without getting his feet wet. But he could also see the damage of the slide, looking like a massive scar through the canyon.

"I would not have wanted to be here when that shit came down" Cal said to him.

"No kidding," Dan agreed. "And it swept all the way down to

the river. It's amazing the creek has dropped this much so quickly."

"Yeah," Cal agreed. "Sure looks passable now."

Dan shook his head. "You should have seen that storm," he said to Cal. "Hail, pouring rain, thunder just exploding all around. And this whole landscape was covered in water, hail, ice. And windy as hell, too."

"Yeah," Cal said dryly. "Sorry I missed that, while I was sitting in my car down at the trailhead."

He was staring at the creek. Then he turned and looked at Dan.

"What do you do when you come to a creek that's too big to cross?" he asked the ranger.

"Look around for another way around—another place to cross," Dan said.

"Upstream or down?" Cal asked.

"Well, usually upstream because it eventually means less water," Dan said. "And in this case, downstream is the Carson River. That's even worse."

"So he goes upstream?" Cal suggested.

Dan glanced up the steep slopes above them near the creek. They were covered with brush. He could see granite boulders poking out between the clumps of manzanita. Some of the boulders were huge. Billowing up in between them, the brush looked like giant pillows. But Dan knew those pillows were a mass of tough branches, dried twigs, and nowhere to put your feet.

"In a massive thunderstorm?" he said to Cal, still staring at the wall of brush.

"What else is he going to do?" Cal asked.

"I can't believe that he'd try going up this," Dan said.

"You're assuming he can see that far," Cal said. "I think he just gets to the creek and turns left." He paused, looking up at the slope above him. "And he goes up because he can't go down."

Dan was still staring uphill. "You want to try and go up this?" he asked.

"No," Cal said. "But don't you think we ought to go see what's up there?"

"I thought you said you had a bad knee," Dan said.

"Yep," Cal said. "I do." And he started up a game trail that snaked up through the manzanita.

Dan watched him climb up for a few seconds, and then followed him.

chapter 42

It was a complete bushwhack.

Dan followed Cal for fifty feet up the hill, then decided that there was a better route off to the left, and soon the two men were lost in their own worlds, crashing through the brush, clambering over fallen logs, working their way around boulders. Always trying to head uphill.

Every once in a while, Dan stopped to take a breath and look around. Usually he caught sight of Cal, or at least his head, working on his own path up the hill. Sometimes he couldn't see Cal, but he could hear him crashing, and sometimes swearing.

"Are you having fun yet?" he called out after hearing a new combination of obscenities.

Cal took a breath. "Do you see anything where you are?" he asked Dan.

"No," Dan admitted.

He had reached the top of a rise and saw now that there was a small ledge of granite that led down to the creek on the right. He figured that if he followed the ledge, it would not only get him over to the creek, but also connect with Cal's chosen path up the hill.

They had now climbed a few hundred yards above the camp, and Dan could see out into the canyon between the trees.

Cal's head was just now visible over the edge of the ledge.

"If he were hiding up here," Dan said, "he'd be able to keep an eye on that whole canyon below. Assuming it wasn't pouring rain."

Dan slowly took in the sights around him. As he faced the canyon, the creek was rushing downhill on his left. Above, a large outcropping of granite towered over him. To the right the forest blocked his view up toward Sonora Peak.

Cal was gasping for breath as he sat down beside Dan.

"Damn, that's hard work," he said. "My knee is killing me."

Dan nodded. His eyes followed the creek as it tumbled down the hillside through the rocks and fallen trees.

"I haven't seen a tree that would get him across the creek," Dan said.

"Maybe he went up further," Cal said. He didn't sound happy about that.

Dan turned and looked up the creek. It didn't look promising, but he could only see a few yards before the rocks and foliage blocked his view.

"It was worth a shot," he said to Cal.

"It would have really been something to be up here during that storm," Cal said. "I bet this creek was like a firehose."

"More like a whole bunch of firehoses," Dan said. He looked across the creek. The going didn't look any easier on that side, either. They were in a small, steep gorge.

"Do you think it would be any easier if we decided to go back down right in the creek bed?" Cal asked.

Dan looked at the jumbled rocks. "Right here it doesn't look too bad," he said. "But if the rocks are slippery, it could get pretty hairy."

Cal looked at Dan and raised his eyebrows. "Want to try it?"

Dan looked at the rocks again, then back at Cal. "Sure. This might be just what you need to fix that knee once and for all."

Cal shrugged. "We can always bail if it gets too hairy."

Slowly Dan picked his way down the chaotic rocks of the gorge. With the stream now a moderate flow, there was room on the side to rock hop along.

This was something he remembered from his childhood, summer afternoons spent trout fishing and rock hopping for days on end. He stepped easily from one rock to the next, never quite stopping, never fully trusting one rock, but always ready to move on to the next one in the sequence. Always looking one or two rocks ahead.

After a few minutes, he realized that he had left Cal far behind. He stopped and waited.

"How are you doing up there?" he asked.

When he didn't get a response from Cal, Dan allowed his mind to worry just a moment.

"Cal?" he called out. "You okay?"

Again, no response.

Dan took a deep breath and started to climb back up the creek bed. It was much harder in this direction.

Above him he heard a faint voice call. "Hey, Dan?"

"Right here!" Dan responded. "On my way."

He looked up to see Cal's face peering down at him from behind a boulder far up the creek.

Dan waved. Cal waved back. "I think you might want to see this," he heard Cal's voice carry down through the gurgling creek.

Cal was signaling something with his hand, but Dan couldn't figure out what it was. So he continued up the creek.

By the time Dan had reached Cal, the deputy was sitting down on a rock. He pointed to a spot below a series of boulders where the creek had widened into a shallow pool. Dan had been grateful for the easy route through here on his way down.

Dan's eyes followed Cal's arm, which was pointing at the far side of the creek. At first he didn't see anything except rocks and roots from the bushes.

Then he saw it. "That's a rope," he said.

"That is a rope," Cal agreed. "If you hadn't been in such a hurry, you probably would have seen it, too."

Dan gave him a quick grin.

"It doesn't look new," Cal said. "But it hasn't been there long. It's not covered in algae or anything."

The rope lay in the deepest part of the creek. Dan's eyes followed it up the creek bed.

"That looks expensive to me," Dan said.

"A climber's rope," Cal agreed. "A couple hundred bucks, easy. Probably more"

"Who leaves a rope like that behind?" Dan asked.

Cal nodded. "Somebody in a hurry," he said. "Or maybe…" he looked downstream.

Dan's eyes followed the rope in the creek.

"It's tied off to that tree up there," Cal said, pointing back upstream.

Dan's eyes followed another thirty or forty feet to see the rope wedged in between rocks at the foot of a substantial tree.

"How far down does it go?" Dan asked.

Cal shrugged. "I tried pulling from up there, but I couldn't budge it. We should probably try down here. But that means somebody is going to have to get their feet wet."

Dan sat down on a rock and started to unlace his boots. "That cold water would be pretty good for your knee," he said.

"I don't want you to see the holes in my socks," Cal answered.

Dan carefully waded out into the creek. The water was only up to his calves at first, but as he waded further into the pool it got deeper. He steadied himself by grabbing an overhead branch.

It took him a minute to focus on the rope again through the water. He reached out with his foot and managed to get his big toe underneath the rope. He gave a tug. The rope seemed to move. He pulled again with his toe and gained some slack.

Hanging on to the branch with both hands, Dan pulled again with his foot, and the end of the rope came free, then rushed back down stream in the current.

"Here," he heard Cal say.

Cal was holding out a four-foot branch toward Dan.

Dan maneuvered the branch under the rope and slowly worked it up to the top of the stream and the current. He dropped the stick and grabbed at the rope.

"Got it!" he yelled.

He turned and slogged through the water toward Cal on the bank. Dan handed the end of the rope to Cal.

When Dan sat down next to him, Cal said, "This rope's been cut."

"How can you tell?" Dan asked.

"First of all, climbing ropes don't break," Cal said. "But look at the end. When a rope like this snaps, it's usually the result of wear and tear—lots of fraying. And the end looks like it. This one is clean. It's been cut."

Dan looked at it. The threads of the rope had begun to unravel in the stream. But they had clearly been cut clean through. He looked at Cal.

"So who cuts an expensive rope like this?" Dan asked. "And

leaves it behind?"

Cal pulled out a long section of the rope and piled it up at his feet on the side of the stream. "There's a good forty or fifty feet of rope here," he said. "If this was a two-hundred-foot rope, they only cut a short piece off."

"Why would you do that?" Dan asked again. "Why not just take it with you?"

"That's one question," Cal admitted. "But I have another one for you."

He looked at Dan, who waited expectantly.

"I wonder what was on the other end," Cal said.

chapter 43

They spent another hour in and around the creek, hoping to find anything that would shed light on the rope. But there was nothing.

They considered trying to pull all the rest of the rope up, but they could see that part of it was buried under a couple of rocks and possibly twisted around some driftwood as well.

"I don't think I get paid enough to do that," Cal had noted. "Maybe you do…"

Dan laughed. "At two bucks a foot, this piece of rope is worth a hundred bucks new," he said. "And two of us have been working on it for more than an hour."

"Let's go work at McDonald's," Cal chuckled. "We'd make more money."

Dan nodded and climbed back up to stand next to Cal. "Anything else to see up here?" he asked.

Cal shook his head.

After another few minutes searching the creek. Dan suggested that they might as well head back down.

"I don't know what else we can do," he said. "Maybe get somebody from your forensics team up here?"

"Not our team," Cal corrected him. "As far as I am concerned, this one has FBI written all over it."

Dan had started to work his way back down the creek again.

"Don't be in too much of a hurry," Cal said. "You might miss something else."

"Yeah, but I'm hungry," Dan said. He turned and hopped down to the next rock.

Dan made an effort to go more slowly, and often stopped to wait for Cal. Cal had picked up another branch, and was using it for a hiking pole as he clambered down the creek.

A few minutes later, Dan stopped to wait for Cal and watch him negotiate a particularly large boulder.

Cal stopped to look at the boulder, and then down to Dan.

"If you stay to the right, there's a smaller rock there that you can just reach with your foot," Dan said.

"My right or your right?" Cal asked.

"Mine," Dan said. "Your left."

Cal looked up at him, and then stopped and stared at something behind Dan.

"We've got company," he said in a quiet voice.

Dan turned around slowly and looked down the gorge. They were now close to the area that Frank Oliver had identified on the photos—a big slide that clearly eroded part of the hillside on the left side of the creek.

And at the bottom of that slide, right where the water roiled up against a large tree trunk, Dan saw the bear.

Dan was always happy to see bears in the mountains. This one was burrowing away at something underneath the log and was oblivious to the two men above.

Dan watched the powerful paws dig into the rocks and dirt by the tree. He swore he could see the tree moving, giving a slight vibration as the bear dug, although the force it took for that to happen was hard to imagine.

"Ow! Fuck!" he heard Cal exclaim from above him. Then a splash.

The bear suddenly stopped digging and looked up. Dan tried hard not to move, not to spook the bear. But behind him Cal had fallen into the creek and was crashing around trying to get out.

The bear watched for only a second, and then resolutely turned and slowly ran right up the side of the hill, right up the freshly eroded hillside.

Dan watched until the bear disappeared from sight over the top of the ridge.

"I'm fine, thanks," he heard Cal say behind him.

"Sorry, but that was really cool," Dan said.

"No, really, I'm fine," Cal repeated. "Glad you got your bear fix."

Dan turned to look at Cal. His friend was dripping wet, and it looked like one of his hands was bleeding.

"That looks painful," Dan said.

Cal blew out his cheeks, then let the air go with a gasp of breath. "I took your advice about my knee," he said. "I gave it a good soaking."

Dan laughed. "Let's get back to camp," he said. "You can get some dry clothes on, and I can get something to eat."

As they walked down the creek, Dan kept an eye out for the bear. It might come back, especially if it had found something good under that log. Or it might just be watching them from somewhere, waiting for them to leave the area so it could return.

Dan made a note to check back later in the day to see if he could catch sight of the bear again.

They were now walking just on the other side of the creek from the tree where the bear had been digging. Dan stared into the water but couldn't see much. And then, as he passed the tree, he saw something that stopped him in his tracks.

Cal, only a few feet behind him, sensed something as well, and stopped right next to Dan.

Dan pointed into the water. This time it was Cal's turn to stare.

Dan looked at Cal, and Cal nodded. "I think we just found the other end of that rope," he said.

Dan walked around on the side of the creek, trying to get a better view of the rope and what might be attached to it.

But Cal had other ideas. He waded right out into the creek and grabbed the rope, pulling hard. It led up underneath the fallen tree.

He pulled it taut and then worked his way up the rope, following it as far as he could.

Once at the tree, Cal bent down and put his head as close to the water as he could without getting it wet. For more than fifteen seconds Dan watched while Cal moved his head slightly from side to side.

Then the deputy reached into the water and grabbed something and gave it a pull.

It didn't budge. Cal pulled again, and lost his footing, slipping down into the water, only his head and one shoulder staying dry. "Shit," the Sheriff said.

"You okay?" Dan called to him.

"I'm great," Cal said disgustedly. He pulled himself back up and reset his feet. This time he gave a mighty pull on the tree, and the whole thing moved slightly.

Dan pulled off his boots and tried to wade over to Cal. But the rocks on the bottom of the stream were too sharp, and he climbed back out of the water to put the boots back on again.

Cal looked over at him. "I think we might be able to roll this tree down into the creek," he said. "When do you think you might be ready to help?"

Dan grinned, but didn't look up. "Be with you in a minute," he called out.

Once his boots were back on, he waded into the creek and joined Cal. The two men stood on the uphill side of the tree and gave a shove. It wiggled, then rolled back into place.

"We need a lever," Dan said.

"Or you could just push a little harder," Cal said. "Let's give it one more try."

Dan looked around for a branch to use as a lever but didn't see one. He bent back over the tree and joined Cal.

"On three," Cal said. "One…two…THREE!"

The tree slowly shuddered and rolled away, then came thundering back towards them.

The two men quickly scrambled out of the way, up the bank.

Dan started laughing. "I'm sure glad there isn't an OSHA inspector around right now," he said.

Cal was already walking back down towards the log. "We can get this," he said. From the sound of his voice, Dan knew Cal was determined not to let the log win.

Resigned, Dan shook his head, then took up a position a little farther up the log.

"You ready?" Cal asked him.

Dan nodded.

"Let's go again," Cal said. "One…two…THREE!"

This time the tree slowly shuddered up, tottered for a moment, and then crashed away with huge splash and rolled down into the creek.

In its wake it left a cloud of muddy water that slowly washed downstream.

As Dan watched the creek wash the mud away he first made out something green, dark green. And then he realized that it was a backpack.

As the two men watched, they could see the water wash away more of the mud. And what came out of the mud was not just a backpack. It was a dark green Kelty backpack.

And it was still attached to a body.

"Sonofabitch," Cal said.

Dan looked around at the mountains towering above him. The sky was that piercing High Sierra blue. He could see a slight breeze gently stroking the trees. The sound of the creek burbled at his feet.

He waded up out of the stream and stood on the bank. Cal was still standing in the water up to his knees, soaked to the skin. He looked at Dan.

Dan sat down on a rock and pulled out his radio.

chapter 44

Dinner at Cal and Maggie's was always a treat, and the fact that Kristen was there made it even better. The smells from the kitchen had them all in a good mood.

In the week since Dan and Cal had found the body, Dan and Kristen had found little time to spend with each other.

That was partly due to the paperwork that Dan had to fill out to report what had happened. That and the debriefings he had to do with the FBI.

For her part, Kristen had spent a couple of days getting all her gear back in order after the base camp fiasco with the biologists. And now that the area was clear, they were talking about going back to finish the job the following Monday.

Maggie called them to the table, and Cal proposed a toast.

"Here's to fifty grand!" he said.

"What?" Kristen said. She looked at Dan, who shared her confusion.

"Didn't you guys hear?" Cal said. "That phone they were looking for was in the backpack. So it turns out that Ranger Dan and I get to split the reward."

"Wow!" Kristen said. "And it's really fifty thousand dollars?"

"Yep," Cal said. "I figure we should probably split it about 75/25, since I was the one who found the rope, and saw the bear, and went into the creek…"

"Cal!" Maggie shouted with disapproval. "It should be fifty-fifty."

Dan laughed. "Actually, Cal, if we're going to be fair, the bear should get a cut. She's the one who found it."

"How do you know it was she?" Maggie asked. "How can you tell?"

"Oh, Dan is on quite familiar terms with most of the bears around here," Cal said. "He's a regular Tarzan of the mountains. First name basis with most of the mama bears."

Dan turned to Cal. "Did you get any more information from the FBI on this whole thing?" he asked.

"The FBI didn't copy me on any memos, if that's what you mean," Cal said.

"But you did hear that they confirmed that the guy we found was who they thought it was, right?" Dan asked.

Cal looked a little uncomfortable. "I guess so…" But he was shaking his head.

"They didn't tell you?" Dan asked. Then he realized that maybe Frank Oliver had shared more with Dan than might have been required. And he wondered how much of that he should talk about here.

"I did see the coroner's report," Cal said. "Well, somebody at the station did. So I know that part."

"What exactly happened?" Kristen asked.

"Based on what we found, and what they learned, it was an ugly way to go," Cal said. "It's all conjecture, but it looks like the guy decided that he was going to try and cross the creek up there where we found the first part of the rope."

"And he tied himself to a tree, to keep from getting washed

downstream?" Dan asked. "Ouch. That almost never turns out well."

"Yep. That's the way it looks," Cal continued. "And from what we can tell, that's just what happened. The guy gets out in the whitewater and his feet go out from under him. He goes downstream. The rope pulls him up short, but now he's stuck in the middle of the rapids and the rope won't let him go anywhere. And he can't even stand up against that current."

"Remember, this creek would have been at full flood stage then," Dan added.

"What did he do?' Kristen asked.

"What we think he did was to cut the rope," said Cal. "At least, that's what it looks like. Only it didn't get better for him, it got worse."

"This is horrible," Maggie said quietly.

"Oh, it was a mess," Cal agreed. "The guy's body was one huge bruise. Two broken legs. Some cracked ribs. A couple of knocks on the head. He got tumbled and crumbled all the way down the creek."

"Okay, that's enough," Maggie said.

"Actually, the lab says that he probably didn't drown," Cal continued. "Looks like maybe hypothermia. So he would have been there a while, probably off to the side somewhere, but he couldn't get out of the water. And then the landslide took care of the rest."

"Okay, please stop now," Maggie insisted.

"An ugly way to go," Cal summed up.

"And they found the phone?' Dan asked.

"Oh yeah," Cal said. "In the backpack. I have no idea if they can ever get it to work, but no, Dan, they did not find the phone."

Dan looked at him quizzically.

"We found the phone," Cal corrected himself. "That's why we get the reward."

"Us and the bear," Dan said.

"Yeah, well, the bear can submit his request in writing," Cal said.

"Or her request," Kristen said. "Dan says it's a her."

chapter 45

After dessert, Dan caught Cal yawning.

"We should go," Kristen suggested.

Dan apologized to Maggie for the dinner conversation. "I usually don't bring my work to dinner with me," he said.

"Oh, Cal does," she answered. "All the time. I've gotten used to it, but it doesn't exactly make for pleasant conversation."

Cal looked down at his shoes.

"Forty-five/forty-five, and we give the bear ten percent," Dan said.

Cal looked at him with an open mouth.

"We can donate ten percent to the Friends of the Forest, in the name of the bear," Dan explained.

Maggie laughed. "Cal wants a fishing boat," she explained. "But I bet there's enough money for the boat and the bear."

Cal did not look happy, but with Maggie on his side, Dan knew he'd won.

After thanking their hosts, Dan and Kristen got into Dan's truck. He'd offered her a ride to and from dinner, and she had accepted.

As they drove off, Kristen turned to Dan.

"You know, Dan, I really want to thank you," she said.

"It's no trouble, I'm happy to do it," he replied.

"No, not for driving," Kristen checked him. "I didn't realize it at the time, but you really went beyond the call of duty up in that canyon. And I wasn't very nice about it at the time."

"Well, you were a little harsh," Dan said. "Did you think I was stalking you or something?"

"I didn't know what to think. The fact is that you surprised me. I was on my way to find a bush…"

Dan was pretty sure that she was blushing.

"Sorry about that," he said. "I was just trying to get there in time."

"I thought you were just showing up to say hello," she said. "I thought you were just showing up for fun. I didn't realize who that guy was, or why you were so concerned. You know, I don't really need a hero on a white horse to rescue me." She looked straight at Dan solemnly. "But I do appreciate what you did."

Dan had no idea what to say to her. He glanced at her. He could tell she was on the verge of tears. Dan took her hand.

"Well, anyway, I would have been much more impressed if I had known all of that at the time," she concluded.

Dan laughed. "Me too," he said. "I'm just glad that it all worked out. None of us got hurt." He thought this over. "Well, nobody but Frank Oliver."

He pulled up the truck in front of Kristen's house.

Kristen undid her seat belt and sat still for the moment.

"Would you like to come in for a cup of coffee?" she asked.

www.ingramcontent.com/pod-product-compliance
Lightning Source LLC
Chambersburg PA
CBHW070752160726
48004CB00001B/159